THREE SLICES

THREE SLICES

novellas of uncanny cheese wizardry

Delilah S. Dawson

Kevin Hearne

Chuck Wendig

Horned Lark Press

This is a work of fiction. All of the characters, organizations, and events portrayed in these stories are either products of the author's imagination or are used fictitiously.

A Horned Lark Press Book
Published by Horned Lark Press
2482 Yonge St. #1087
Toronto, ON M4P 2H5

www.hornedlarkpress.com

First Edition
ISBN: 978-1-998390-06-9

Printed in a Secret Volcano Lair by Antifascist Capybaras

BY DELILAH S. DAWSON

The Violence

Bloom

Midnight at the Houdini

Mine

Camp Scare

Servants of the Storm

THE SHADOW SERIES, WRITTEN AS LILA BOWEN

Wake of Vultures

Conspiracy of Ravens

Malice of Crows

Treason of Hawks

THE HIT SERIES

Hit

Strike

THE BLUD SERIES

Wicked as They Come

Wicked as She Wants

Wicked After Midnight

Wicked Ever After

Star Wars

Inquisitor: Rise of the Red Blade

Galaxy's Edge: Black Spire

Phasma

The Skywalker Saga

The Minecraft Mob Squad Series

Minecraft: Mob Squad

Minecraft: Never Say Nether

Minecraft: Don't Fear the Creeper

Disney Mirrorverse: Pure of Heart

Creator-Owned Comics

Ladycastle

Sparrowhawk

Star Pig

www.delilahsdawson.com

BY KEVIN HEARNE

BY CHUCK WENDIG

Black River Orchard

The Book of Accidents

Zer0es

Invasive

Dust & Grim

You Can Do Anything, Magic Skeleton

Wanderers Duology

Wanderers

Wayward

Miriam Black

Blackbirds

Mockingbird

The Cormorant

Thunderbird

The Raptor & The Wren

Vultures

The Heartland trilogy

Under the Empyrean Sky

Blightborn

The Harvest

Atlanta Burns

Atlanta Burns

Atlanta Burns: The Hunt

Non-Fiction

The Kick-Ass Writer

Damn Fine Story

Gentle Writing Advice

Star Wars

Aftermath

Life Debt

Empire's End

Mookie Pearl

The Blue Blazes

The Hellsblood Bride

www.terribleminds.com

AUTHORS' NOTES

Kevin

I can't recall precisely *where* I heard that tyromancy was actually a thing, but methinks it was during the summer of 2012. As soon as I knew it existed, I knew I had to write about it, the way some people have to climb mountains or crack safes once they see them. And if I could find another couple of authors brave enough to do it, maybe we could produce the world's first tyromancy-themed anthology. So my quest began, and now here is the spiffy MacGuffin: THREE SLICES, or rather three stories where somebody along the way predicts the future via the coagulation of cheese. I couldn't be more thrilled to share this volume with Delilah S. Dawson and Chuck Wendig, authors whose work I admire and humans I am proud to call my friends.

And I am super-mega-turbo-chuffed that Galen Dara agreed to illustrate this for us as well. All three of us are huge fans of her work and she makes us geek out.

My novella, *A Prelude to War*, is a vital part of the Iron Druid Chronicles—fans of the series should consider it IDC

7.5. For that reason it might not be the ideal introduction to my work; if you like to read series in order then please begin with *Hounded,* book 1.

Many thanks to my Metal Editor, Tricia Narwani, for her usual sterling insights, and to Richard Shealy for copy edits.

Hope you enjoy!

Delilah

When Kevin Hearne says, "Hey, do you want to do an anthology?" you say YES. And when you find out it's about tyromancy, and that Chuck Wendig is also involved and that Galen Dara is doing the art, you know you made the right decision. That's my life philosophy: Always say yes to cheese.

When I asked my readers what they'd most like in a short story, the unanimous answer was MORE CRIMINY, which is why this is my first Blud story from a man's perspective. But you don't need to have read the books to enjoy it, and I hope you'll consider it a welcoming introduction to the dark, dangerous, whimsical world of Sang, where tyromancy fits in perfectly.

So thank you, Kevin and Chuck, for squishing my story between your words like the buttercream in a birthday cake. Thanks to Tricia and Shecky for embettering that story and for Galen to bringing together my favorite things in her illustration: vampire horses, blood, and dangerous chicks with lassoes. And thank you, dear reader, for joining us in this mad world of cheese and prognostication.

Chuck

It was only a matter of time before we played straight down the middle and decided to aim for the popular crowd and write a series of novellas based on tyromancy. All the cool kids are doing it. Flannery O'Connor. Stephen King. Pat Rothfuss. We are nothing if not bandwagoneers, and we want a slice (get it? Slice?) of that sweet, sweet cheese-reader money.

Which means, most of all, I need to thank you readers for reading this in the first place. Deciding to take a risk on *yet another* tyromancy cheese-story collection is kind of you. And I know we all appreciate it.

Big ups too to my fellow anthology mates here—Delilah S. Dawson and Kevin Hearne are that rare combination of *incredibly nice* and *incredibly talented*, and so it is my distinct privilege to be here with them now.

Also, thanks to Shecky for the copy-edits, Tricia for the big edits, and Galen Dara who remains one of my favorite artists working in SFF today.

A PRELUDE TO WAR
Iron Druid Chronicles 7.5

Kevin Hearne

The events of this story take place a week to ten days after the events of Shattered, *book 7 of the Iron Druid Chronicles*

The lowland marsh in the hours before dawn was perhaps a bit too quiet. The rasp of insects and the throaty warbles of amphibians, so raucous moments before, had fallen off into nervous titters, and it wasn't because of my presence or because of Oberon's. We weren't the predators here. I crouched down next to my hound in the tall grass and put a hand on the back of his neck. Not wanting to alert whoever might be listening with my speech, I spoke to him through the mental bond we shared.

Quietly now. We are being stalked.

<By what?>

I imagine we'll find out soon enough when it jumps on us.

<When it—? That's not your plan, is it? Wait and let it jump on us?>

My plan was not to be prey at any point, but things with teeth and an appetite usually get to decide what's for dinner.

<Nah, come on, Atticus! Do that Druid thing you do. Talk to the elemental and have it tell the hungry things to eat something else.>

That would be cheating.

Oberon's head began to swivel back and forth, searching for anything approaching through the reedy grasses that grew waist-high around puddles of standing water. <I hope you will not be disappointed in my lack of moral fiber, Atticus, but I am all for cheating when it comes to not being eaten.>

We need to get our senses back into shape, Oberon, and here nature has provided us an opportunity to test ourselves. Nothing better for your hearing than being prey instead of predator for a while.

<First, my senses are just fine. Second, why do we have to do it here? Can't we do one of those fun zombie runs instead where they don't really eat your brains, they just chase you with a lot of makeup on?>

I told you already. We have to see somebody here and this is where she lives.

We were in Ethiopia, the far western portion of it bordering Sudan, in a wilderness now known as Gambela National Park. Most of it was grassland and low-lying wetlands like this, but the occasional tree-covered ridge would rise up as a pro-forma nod to topography and varied ecology. Lots of African buffalo and large antelope species like hartebeests and kob grazed in the area. Prides of lions and other big cats ran around grazing on them, and vultures grazed on the leftovers.

<Oh yeah. The fortune-teller. I have a question about that. What if she wakes up at dawn and sees in her magic runes or whatever that she's going to tell our fortune today except that we get eaten before we get there so that means her schedule is free and then her runes don't know what to say except "Hey, how about those Broncos?">

What? Oberon, that is the most bizarre hypothetical ever. She doesn't even use runes.

<Well, you made me nervous. And you didn't answer my question.>

The answer is divination doesn't work like that. It doesn't tell you that a certain future got canceled and it doesn't make small talk. If it reveals anything, it reveals the most likely of futures, and that's always up to interpretation. Even if you get the interpretation right, it can still change due to circumstances. You remember what Master Yoda said about the future?

<It's always in motion. Difficult to see.>

That's right. Come on, let's keep moving, but keep an eye out and your nose in the wind.

<All right, but I still think you should cheat. I don't want to be a part of the circle of life here. Hey, speaking of which,

is this the stretch of Africa where meerkats hang out with warthogs and sing cheerful songs about stress-free living?>

Tell you what. If you see them, I'll let you join in.

<Aces.>

We crept as best as we could through the marsh; my feet would occasionally make squidgy noises in the sucking mud, and without the covering drone of the local fauna, it sounded abnormally loud. I was grateful that we had a blanket of darkness to disguise us.

I had cast night vision on us both so that we could see well, and we were alert for any noise above the swish of our own passage. Something else was alert to us.

Hey, Oberon. I'll bet you a sausage it's a cheetah.

<No way! The last time I bet sausage and lost, you ate it in front of me and made yummy noises. I still have nightmares about the Sausage That Got Away. And besides, you probably already know what's after us.>

I swear I don't. I'm not cheating. You will probably figure it out before I do just based on what you smell.

<So far, I just smell us and funky marsh. No, wait! Atticus, I smell something dead—>

That was all the warning I got before a vampire leapt at me out of the grass from the left, arms outstretched, and tackled me into the mire. I threw up a forearm to prevent access to my throat but couldn't manage anything else, as my sword arm was trapped beneath me. I got fangs in my arm and long, sharp nails digging into my shoulders.

<Atticus!>

Stay back, Oberon! A vampire would kill him without a thought and I didn't want to give him the chance, especially when I might be able to kill the vampire with nothing more than a thought. Since vampires weren't living creatures, Gaia let us unbind them to their component parts. The trick to it was staying alive long enough to speak the unbinding. I'd almost died that way at the hands and fangs of a vampire almost as old as I was. Since then, I'd been working on a charm like the others around my neck that would execute a binding via mental command. The problem was, I had so few vampires to practice on to perfect it.

Granuaile, my partner, asked me why I couldn't simply practice on dead bodies, since that's essentially what vampires were.

"They're a bit more than that, though," I replied. "A mere dead body doesn't walk around and consume blood. Vampires have magic to them that gives their bodies animation and strength, and that gray aura with the two red power centers in the head and heart. You have to unbind that as well as the raw matter of the body. That's in the Old Irish words of the spell, remember—it attacks their magic first and *then* their bodies so that the magic cannot rebind to them. So, I need real vampires to practice on if I want to make this work."

On my single previous attempt, I'd caused the targeted vampire to experience something akin to mild digestive discomfort. He looked surprised but not especially pained. That had been encouraging, though—the targeting was working, at least, and having some effect. I'd adjusted the binding and craftsmanship of the charm since then and hoped it would work now. I triggered it as the vampire withdrew his fangs from my arm and dove again for my throat. The spell hit him like a punch to the solar plexus.

He coughed blood and convulsed, his eyes squeezing shut for a second and then opening wide in surprise. He clutched his chest like he was having a heart attack, and I was able to push him off and roll away, muttering the words to the unbinding. The vampire recovered quickly and got up in time to launch himself at me once more, but now I had my guard up and I wasn't going down again. I sidestepped his charge and finished the unbinding, after which he came apart with a splash inside his clothes and his head exploded into a mist of blood and bone dust.

<Okay, that was kind of awesome. You know how many hits we'd get on YouTube if we caught that on video?>

A better question would be "What's a vampire doing out here?" Or maybe how I'd get clean anytime soon. I was covered in mud, which tended to happen when you rolled around in it, and I had some wounds that needed healing; I tripped my healing charm and let Gaia get to work on me.

<I was going to ask that next. After I asked if you're okay.>

Yeah, thanks, I'm all right. His bite will heal up quickly. But we'd better move a bit faster ourselves. I'm worried about Mekera now.

And my charm wasn't quite there yet. It had clearly impacted the power center around the vampire's heart but hadn't destroyed it, and nothing happened to his head until I completed the full unbinding verbally. I would just have to keep working on it. Changing a structured verbal unbinding to a mental one in close proximity to the cold iron of my amulet was so tricky that it usually took me years to perfect a charm.

Keep your nose open for more vampires, I told Oberon, *but let's pick up the pace a little.*

My hound easily lengthened his stride to match mine and we emerged from the marsh into a slightly dryer grassland that would, at a higher elevation, turn into a shrubby savanna. It had been so long since I'd been to this part of the world that there were few tethered trees nearby, and the Fae rangers had apparently ignored their duties here to some extent, necessitating a long run to our destination.

Mekera lived off the grid by choice. She'd tried modern conveniences and said, "Yep, that's convenient," but pointed out that all electricity did was keep her in cities around lots of other people, and she liked her people in very small doses. After World War II and the Italian occupation of Ethiopia, she didn't even want a small dose—I think something happened to her during that time, and I missed it since I'd been busy in the French Pyrenees helping people escape the Third Reich. She wouldn't talk about it when I came to visit her, either. I got the sense from her glare that she couldn't believe that the world had come to ask one more thing of her. But since I was one of the few people who could grant a particular wish of hers, she offered me a deal: Set her up someplace where she could do the hermit thing right for a while, and she'd practice her art on my behalf, predicting the safest places in the world to hide from Aenghus Óg in the coming decades. A lone rocky outcropping in the middle of the savanna, a sort of rebel hill that looked down on herds of ruminants, practically begged to be a secret lair. And so, with the help of the local elemental, I created one for her, carving an entrance out of the rock that would be invisible from the air and provide her with a shaded front porch. Everything else was underground, cool and sealed with nonporous stone so that she didn't get flooded during the rainy season. She had a well of clear, clean water, the bottom level of her hideaway was cold enough to keep her perishables safe, and she did quite well for herself.

In the nineties, before I moved to Tempe and adopted Oberon, she gave in to modernity and sent me a letter in San Diego—a feat in itself, since I had only been there a couple weeks and told no one where I was—asking me to upgrade her place with electricity. She wanted a stove and some other modern accouterments and needed windmills to make it happen. It was a challenging project to create a functional kitchen and laboratory for her, but thoroughly enjoyable. Especially since my reward for this work was a precise divination on where to find my best friend. I had spent too long without an animal companion and felt it was time to do things right with a hound. Without a friend to trust you could sour on modern life, sour on the world, and withdraw from it like Mekera had.

"There is an Irish wolfhound rescue ranch in Massachusetts," she told me back then, when the United States was consumed with its president's infidelities. "And if you arrive there on this precise date, you will catch him immediately after he arrives."

That last part was important because rescue ranches always spay and neuter the animals they take in. I caught Oberon before his trip to the vet, and Granuaile similarly caught Orlaith before she could be spayed. The two of them would have puppies someday and I was looking forward to it.

I'd never told Oberon how I'd come to find him there or what fate awaited him had I been a day or two later. I figured he would have nightmares about it.

Even though it was early morning and the sky was still gray with only the barest hint of sunrise, Mekera was sitting outside in a sling chair when we arrived on her front stoop, our chests heaving from a pleasant run unaided by the earth.

"Hello, Mekera."

There was no welcome for an old acquaintance in her expression, and her voice was sullen. "Huh. Thought you'd be along sooner rather than later. Maybe not covered in mud, but still: good timing. The coffee's almost ready. And there's cheese and injera if you're hungry," she said, referring to a sourdough flatbread popular in Ethiopia. She rose from her chair, dressed in a long white linen tunic that split at the sides past her hips, with a two-inch-wide band of green and gold embroidery around the neck that met in the middle, fell in a single strip down to her knees, and then exploded into an Abyssinian cross design. It was a style of clothing favored by Habesha people, who were among the world's first converts to Christianity long ago. Mekera had at one time been a *debtera* in the Ethiopian Orthodox Tewahedo Church, though I think she gave that up at the beginning of the twentieth century. She kept her hair natural and maintained the appearance of a woman in her forties. She had something like khakis tucked into worn and scuffed calf-high, dark brown boots that she wore as low-grade armor against snakebites. She paused with her hand on the door handle and glanced back at Oberon. "Big dog. That the one I told you about last time I saw you?"

"Yes."

"He won't be eating my breakfast or peeing on it, will he?"

"No. He's very well-behaved."

<What? I don't have to be well-behaved for that! Who pees on breakfast, Atticus? What kind of dog would ever—wait. Are there dogs like that nearby? Defilers of breakfast?>

I'm sure there are wild dogs about. Not sure if they're that wild, though.

"Well, come on in and sit down, then," Mekera said, pulling open the steel door and audibly releasing a puff of coffee-scented air from inside.

<Did I hear her say she told you about me?>

Yes. She's the reason I found you when I did.

<Oh! Well then, I definitely won't pee on anything.>

We followed her down a stairway into the main living area, which was comprised of a stone table and four wooden chairs I had bound together myself, and which led to the kitchen that I had expanded in the nineties to include modern appliances. She still had a stock of candles, I saw, but had switched to lamps with high-efficiency bulbs for the majority of her illumination.

"You were expecting me?" I asked, washing mud off my hands and arms in her sink while she poured coffee. We both took it black.

"Yes," she said, and then took the mugs over to her table and waited for me there while I dried off with a kitchen towel. We took appreciative first sips before she continued. "I didn't see you in a divination, though—it was just a logical probability based on past events. Did you catch the thrall outside?"

I frowned at her. "No. What thrall?"

"The vampire thrall. He's been stalking me despite my strict no-stalking policy. Watches me during the day. Watches my door, anyway. Probably saw you come in here."

"No, I didn't see him," I said, cursing myself for not being more cautious in my approach. "But I think we got the vampire before dawn—that's why we're muddy."

An eyebrow rose on Mekera's face to indicate mild surprise. "You got the vampire? Well, it won't matter. The thrall will call you in and we'll have a whole bunch more vampires here before the night is through. Probably just saw my last sunrise. It's no wonder I couldn't see what was going to happen today with you around. That amulet of yours messes everything up."

"I know. That's partly why I'm here. I don't trust my own divination anymore. I was never terribly good at it to begin with."

Mekera pointed with a finger at the base of my throat. "It's that cold iron. Don't you ever take it off?"

"I can, but then I have to forgo its protection. Risky business for me these days. And since I'd like to know about my own future and I'll certainly be wearing it in the future—"

"You can't rely on what you see while you don't have it on," Mekera finished.

"Right."

"You came a long way to get your fortune told, my friend. All the soothsayers on the other side of the planet too busy?"

I'd been listening to the Morrigan most recently, but she was gone, and the situation amongst the Tuatha Dé Danann right now was less than optimal. "I don't trust them."

"Huh. Meaning you trust me? You shouldn't."

"Why not? That tip you gave me in the sixteenth century regarding coffee as the next big commodity was spot-on." I jabbed a finger at my mug. "This made me the bulk of my fortune. I was the world's quietest coffee baron."

Mekera grunted. "That so? And what happened to all that fortune?"

"It's a long story, but a man named Werner Drasche got access to my accounts and liquidated them. The money's all gone."

"Don't have to tell me the story. I already know it. I'm the one who told him to go after Kodiak Black if he wanted to get to you." I flinched and a cold feeling collected in the pit of my stomach.

Kodiak Black and I had enjoyed a very long friendship. He was one of my oldest friends, in fact; I met him before most of the Old World had heard there was a New World. He spent summers as an enormous bear and the rest of the year as a human, what he called his hibernation. When the continent began filling up with people who weren't so careful or considerate of nature, I did what I could to make sure the salmon runs he adored in Alaska remained open and unpolluted, and he looked after the majority of my finances as that became a project worthy of a custodian. He got killed for managing my money, though, and in a way that made me shudder for his spirit. I had serious doubts that his spirit existed anymore, for the very life had been drained out of him by Werner Drasche, the arcane lifeleech.

"Told you," Mekera said, "I'm not to be trusted."

"You betrayed me?"

That earned me a sneer. "I was never loyal to you in the first place. But hell yes."

"Why? What did I do?"

"Not a damn thing, Siodhachan. Look, it's not like I was out to get you. That crazy ascot-wearing fool was going to kill me. Came here with his own private nest of vampires and all of them looked at me like I was a snack. They were watching—listening—and they would have known if I was lying. I had to do it out of self-preservation. Did he kill Kodiak?"

"Yes."

She dropped her head and said in a low voice, "I'm very sorry to hear that. He didn't need to go that far."

I let that obvious statement pass without comment. "Why'd he let you live after you helped him? That doesn't sound like Drasche's style."

Mekera looked up. "He thought you might come looking for me afterward, and then he'd have you. And look!" Her eyes widened in mock surprise and she spread her hands like a game show hostess. "Here you are!"

I flicked a nervous glance toward the entrance. "Drasche's out there now?"

"Nah, but you can bet he will be soon enough."

"We can be long gone before then."

"You and the hound? I know. Doesn't help me."

"I was including you. You can come with us."

"But I like it here. Got my lab and my sky and no junk mail. Don't want to move."

"Fine, stay here if you want. But what you did to me—what you did to Kodiak—you need to make it right."

Her eyes flashed and she stabbed a finger at me. "I didn't do anything to you or Kodiak. That lifeleech threw down all the evil here. All I did was save my own ass and I don't owe you anything for that. You want to talk about betrayal? Ask yourself how Drasche knew where to find me."

"I didn't tell him."

"I wasn't suggesting that. I'm saying somebody you know sent him after me."

"Who?" I said, already dreading the answer.

"Leif Helgarson."

"Damn it." I ground my teeth together, clenched my fists, and asked, "But how did he know you were here?"

"He found me in ninety-five; don't know precisely how. Told me he'd been seeking out the world's best soothsayers to figure out where he could find the world's last Druid."

"And he threatened you just like Drasche did, so you told him I'd most likely be in Arizona in the late nineties."

"Tempe, to be exact. Didn't know if you'd actually show up or not. But he didn't threaten me. He straight-up laid down a glamour and I spilled."

It was facepalm time for me, because I remembered Leif spinning a tale about meeting Flidais in the eighteenth century and waiting for me to arrive "in the desert" based on her advice. I swallowed it at the time because I was so intent on keeping a promise to him that I couldn't accept that he was playing me. Now, though, I can see it for the bullshit that it was. Flidais wouldn't have told him a thing—she'd have unbound him on general principle if she ever met him. But with Mekera's information, he could go to Tempe, ingratiate himself with the werewolf pack there, and wait for me to show up and make courtesy contact with them.

This meant that Drasche and Leif were still on speaking terms. Conspiring terms, even. I thought that I had managed to set Drasche against Leif back in France, but apparently I hadn't sown enough doubt. Or, more likely, Leif was simply better than I was at manipulating people. I wondered now if his ignorance of language was all feigned, a device he used to humanize himself. He would have taken issue with Mekera's use of "straight-up laid down," for example, and I would have felt superior in explaining it to him, when it was all part of his long con.

"Why did *he* leave you alive?" I asked. "You could have warned me. You *should* have warned me when I came to fix up your place and you told me where to find Oberon."

"Told him the same thing I told you: I don't owe you anything. I look out for myself. And he said he could appreciate that."

"I bet he did."

"And he also said he'd find me again if you didn't show up by the millennium."

"Ah, there was the threat."

"But it just so happens," she continued, her hand spreading out like a stop sign, "that my ass needs saving again and I probably can't talk my way out of it this time. So, whatever you're wanting me to divine for you, I'll do it if you protect me from Werner Drasche and the vampires until you've killed them all. Because that's what you're aiming to do, right?"

I stared at her in shocked disbelief. "I can't believe you're asking for a favor now when you've just admitted to selling me out *twice*."

"I'm not asking for a favor. I'm naming the price for my services, and my services are worth it. I helped you find your dog there and kept you away from that god you were running from, didn't I?"

"Aenghus Óg found me in Tempe," I pointed out.

"Only because you stayed too long." She closed one eye and cocked a finger at me. "I told you ten years and you pushed it, didn't you?" I sighed in defeat because I did stay there longer than I should have. "All right, then. I'll tell you the future and you be my shield."

"I can agree with that in the abstract," I said, "but I honestly can't protect you here. Best I can do is take you somewhere they won't be able to reach you until it's all over, then bring you back."

She narrowed her eyes, wary of a trick. "This is someplace nice you're talking about? Not a hole in a city somewhere?"

"Oh, yes. It can be very nice. I can take you to a different plane if you want."

"Which plane?"

I paused to consider where she'd be both safe and free from harassment. "How about Emhain Ablach, one of the Irish planes? It means the Isle of Apples. No vampires there. No lifeleeches, either. Not even junk mail." And almost no faeries except for the seagoing kind. It was Manannan Mac Lir's bailiwick and very few Fae visited it unless they had his permission. He wouldn't mind having a special guest there for a while.

"What about people? Or your Irish gods?"

"No people. The god doesn't visit often and I'll make sure he's okay with you staying there. You might see some selkies, but they won't mess with you."

"That does sounds pleasant. All right, it's a deal, if we live long enough to get the tyromancy done. You're out for blood, so you need a blood cheese."

"Pardon me?"

Oberon needed to weigh in at the mention of food. <Atticus, that sounds illegal. Or non-kosher. I forget which.>

How do you know about kosher?

<I saw it on a television show. It was something about never mixing meat and dairy. Blood in your cheese sounds like a violation of that.>

"I mean I'm going to have to use rennet derived from an animal rather than what I normally use to curdle the milk," Mekera said. "As a rule, I use rennet derived from mallow. So we're going to have to go hunting."

<Hunting sounds good! But how did we get there from blood cheese? Either this lady is extremely weird or I missed something.>

I'll explain as we go. I said to Mekera, "You don't have any rennet available?"

"Not the kind I need for the tyromancy you want. We should get a kid hartebeest. I have the milk already."

<Did she just say she has hartebeest milk?>

Yes. You need rennet specific to the milk; sheep's rennet won't work as well on cow's milk, or vice versa.

<But how did she milk a hartebeest?>

That's the kind of mystery I'd prefer not to solve.

"Okay," I said, "if that's what we need to do, let's do it."

She finished her coffee, rose, and strapped on a belt with a large hunting knife that hung on a hook by the ladder to the exit. "I don't need to bring my bow, do I? You'll bring the animal down?"

"Yeah, we'll take care of it," I said. "You know where to find them?"

She snorted. "I've been living here since 1945, remember?"

"Fair enough." I frowned as she turned away, the length of that time span finally hitting me. That was a lifetime of living alone, and she still wasn't sick of it—she wanted even more solitude.

Mekera rummaged in a cupboard until she found a box of freezer bags, then she took one, folded it, and tucked it into her belt next to the knife scabbard. "The hartebeest are a few miles to the north," she said. "We could walk it if you want, or if you're in a hurry, you could give me a ride." She smiled at me for the first time and I shook my head. She wanted me to change into a stag and let her ride on my back, but I thought she'd already taken me for a ride too many.

"We'll run as we are and I'll feed you energy to keep your strength up," I said.

Her smile disappeared and she shrugged. "Suit yourself."

The run to the north took an hour, even with me boosting our speed via bindings, but eventually we topped a knoll with knee-high grasses and looked down on plain full of grazing antelope. More than a hundred animals roamed there, and sentinels on the edges looked out for predators like us. There were a few kids, I noted, which is what we wanted.

"There you are, boys," Mekera said. "There will be hyenas around and vultures soon enough. Might even be a lion. As soon as you bring one down, you'll have to guard the kill until I get there and harvest the stomach."

I slid my eyes sideways. "Now that you mention it, how are you going to get to it safely with all those hungry things looking around for something slow to eat?"

Mekera's eyes shifted to meet mine. "You'll have the elemental make them look somewhere else, of course."

<Ha! You're going to have to cheat now, Atticus.>

I suppose I will.

I have never been a proponent of any kind of divination that demands blood—that's why I use wands or augury—but sometimes magic demands that price, and weaker forms of divination wouldn't serve me well now. At least in this case, nothing would be wasted; whatever we didn't use would feed the food chain here.

"Please hold on to my clothes," I said, stripping down and folding them up. "I'll tell the elemental to watch out for you. You can follow behind us as soon as we take off."

Mekera only nodded in response and wordlessly accepted my jeans and shirt before I bound my shape to that of a wolfhound. I didn't feel comfortable leaving Fragarach behind when there might be a vampiric thrall about, so I took it into my mouth and told Oberon I'd flush one to him and he'd have to do the actual killing.

<That sounds good to me, Atticus.>

I reminded him that this was going to be quite different from hunting a single deer or a small herd like we usually did, my mental voice slightly altered by my shift to a hound. <There's a hundred of them and only two of us,> I said, <and they have horns.>

<I know; I'll watch for sudden turns.>

<We have to make this fast, too. We have a short window of time to accomplish what we need to do here.>

<Got it.>

<And watch out for other predators that might want to join in or swoop in and steal your kill. The savanna is cutthroat like that.>

<Eyes and ears and nose wide open, Atticus,> my hound said.

<All right, then, let's hunt.>

We sprinted away together through the tall grass, gray ridges of fur slicing across the top of the growth toward our prey.

'm reevaluating my weapons after that battle in Tír na nÓg against Fand and the Fae. At one point, I had grabbed an axe embedded in Atticus's arm and tossed it at a goblin. It took him out instantly—no twitching, no last desperate swing at me—he was simply done. It's gotten me thinking. Had I thrown an axe instead of a knife at Fand, we might have ended the whole battle before it truly started. But there had been good reasons, during my training, to stick with knives instead of heavier weapons. I could carry and throw far more of them than I could axes, and I also turned out to have good aim and simply preferred them. Atticus had me train with axes somewhat—he had me try almost everything at least once—but I set them aside in favor of knives because knives would allow me to draw, throw, and return quickly to a two-handed grip on my staff. I truly relished the smash-'n-poke action of Scáthmhaide, and I had thought that committing to anything larger than a knife would mean I had to forgo many of its advantages.

But now I'm thinking differently: Why can't I keep the knives and simply add an axe? For those times when you absolutely, positively have to bring a mofo down from a distance without a firearm, an axe designed in the tomahawk style—that is, a single-bladed hand axe ideal for throwing— would serve me much better than a knife, especially against armor; the force I could bring to bear behind an axe head was much greater than a knife's point.

Firearms would work too, of course, but I like being able walk around in public with my staff and have people think I'm a harmless if quirky personality instead of a potential mass murderer. Adding an axe wouldn't be that strange; I live in the forest above Ouray and a hand axe would be endlessly useful. Everybody would think, "That's for firewood" and not "That's for skulls."

Atticus is trying to track down Werner Drasche, and once he does, I think we're going to have a double-XL ruckus. He's been financing a shadow war against the vampires using mercenary yewmen, and the vampires sent their toady to hit one of his friends in retaliation. Neither side will back down now and the argument will be settled, as so many arguments have, through violence. So, since it's just me and Orlaith at the cabin now, it would behoove me to use the time to up my game.

I've collected several different models of "hawks," as enthusiasts like to call them these days, to experiment and see which kind would suit me best. Some have longer handles than others and different heads on them, and this of course makes their weight and balance vary from axe to axe. My concern is not weight so much as whether they fly true and rotate well after release. The axe must rotate at least once midflight before striking, and judging the distance required for that to happen is often the key to making a lethal throw. Longer throws with multiple revolutions are too easy to dodge, too often hit on the handle instead of the blade, and are rarely accurate—I remember laughing at the circus throws Orlando Bloom's character made in those pirate movies.

At first, I'm partial to metal handles because I remember how effective the Black Axes of the Norse dwarfs were in Hel against the *draugr*, and their smaller, blocking axes were all metal, but to my mind, they don't throw as well as the hawks with wooden handles. I have my unbreakable staff to block, anyway; what I need is an accurate throw.

My targets are made from fallen branches and firewood since I can't countenance using a living tree for target practice. Crafting them is a good exercise for me too: I keep the cellulose of the wood but unbind the current structure and rebind and reshape it into a sort of Druidic plywood, which I set up at the base of trees in a course through our woods. And then I go coursing with Orlaith, carrying a sack full of different hawks in my left hand and chucking them at targets on the run to test their feel and my aim. Orlaith is careful to run a couple steps behind me on my left side, never getting in the line of fire. I invite her to talk to me as we run, which tests her language skills and distracts me as well, a necessary component since battles are almost entirely composed of distractions. If you can't focus on a target while being distracted, you will die.

<I am getting better with my language, Granuaile. See? I said all my verbs right in that sentence!>

You did in your first sentence, indeed. You are such a smart hound.

<Did I say mistake in my other sentence?>

A very tiny one. You modify verbs with adverbs instead of adjectives, so it would have been better to say "correctly" instead of "right," but your meaning was clear. You are improving quickly and I am proud of you.

<Does that mean I talk with Oberon soon?>

I smile because I had seen that question coming a long way off. Oberon constantly asks me too if Orlaith is ready to be bound yet. I know he pesters Atticus about it as well, but he always deflects and says it's my decision, which means that both hounds ask me when we will bind their minds together multiple times per day, sometimes only minutes apart because they are so bad at remembering how long it was since they last asked.

Part of me recognizes that she is ready now. She can follow my conversation easily and her fluency is improving daily. But I don't want her to feel intimidated by Oberon's abilities. He's a very old hound with many more years of practice at language, and since he's male and smitten, he will try to impress her from the start, and I want Orlaith to be able to hold her own.

I admit there is probably an element of selfishness to it; I enjoy having Orlaith all to myself. But she is so smart that soon I will have no excuse to keep them apart.

When I think you are ready, we will bind your minds together, I tell her, as I have told her already numerous times. *You can trust me on that.*

<I know I can trust you.>

I mentally smile at her and then focus on my practice. Whether it is a function of their manufacture or a function of my throwing mechanics, I confirm that the wooden hawks fly better than the all-metal ones. One particular model with a twenty-two inch handle seems close to perfect but not quite there. I shave a half-inch off the bottom of the handle and try it, and it's closer. After I shave another half-inch off the bottom, it's perfect for me. I'm hitting targets consistently on the run at varying distances. Satisfied, I make a note to order more and spend some time practicing melee combo moves with my staff in my left hand. Gandalf made a sword-and-staff dual wield look badass in *Return of the King*, but working with a hawk is an entirely different proposition because there are no stabbing moves.

It's while I'm working through how to deal with an opponent holding a longsword that my mind returns to the indelible mark on my left biceps. It's because Loki wields a longsword that I'm reminded of him and the brand he left on my skin, and I cannot heal that mark with Druidry. Gaia doesn't even recognize that there's a problem. I've healed from the broken bones and my bruises are all gone now, but that mark remains, and it means he knows where I am at all times while hiding me from the sight of all others. The latter is a definite plus, but the cost is that Loki holds a certain power over me, and that I cannot abide—especially since he strongly hinted he would try to use me again to advance his goals. I owe him a death in return for my father's, and many broken bones before that. Atticus has his vengeance to exact for his friend, and I have my own to pursue.

The nature of Loki's magic is Norse; the mark is made of runes. What if…

<Granuaile? What is wrong? Why did you stop?> Orlaith asks me, and I turn my head to look at her. She had lain down in the leaves, head on her paws, watching me train, but now her head is up and her ears cocked in a query.

"What if Odin could get rid of Loki's mark for me?" I say aloud.

<Who's Odin?>

"Loki's father—well, he adopted Loki, but still. If anyone could undo a Norse binding, it would be him, and I bet he doesn't even know Loki is doing this."

<Great! Let's go ask him! Where does he live?>

"In Asgard. I don't have a good way of getting there." Atticus had shifted to the Norse plane and then climbed the trunk of Yggdrasil to get to Asgard, but that path was surely blocked now that the Æsir knew about it.

<Maybe call him on your phone?>

"I don't think Odin has a phone. And there's no cell service in Asgard, anyway. But you know, there might be a different way to get in touch. Ready for a run?"

<Okay! Where do we go?>

"Just down the hill."

Our cabin is about a mile uphill from the Camp Bird Mine foreman's house along County Road 26. Atticus and I met Frigg there once, and Odin's ravens, Hugin and Munin, had been there as well. Odin knew the precise location of our cabin too, of course; Atticus once left Odin's spear, Gungnir, inside for him to pick up. But the foreman's house, being unoccupied, might be more neutral ground, and since Frigg and the dwarven Runeskald Fjalar had spent some time fixing up the place into a sort of mead hall, they might still have an affinity for it that I can use.

The foreman's house is more of a white Colonial mansion, and when we reach it, the exterior still looks dilapidated and afflicted with all the ills of age and inclement weather, complete with peeling paint, a sagging front porch, and boarded-up windows. Hugin and Munin are not conveniently perched outside waiting to bear Odin a message, unfortunately, so I have to devote some thought to how I might contact him.

I have no idea whether he would respond to a prayer. Do the prayers of nonbelievers ever reach the gods, or are they automatically screened by faith and fervor? Atticus never covered details like this in my training, and it's not the sort of thing I would have thought to ask him—"Hey, Atticus, how do I get in touch with Odin in case I need to chat?"

Seeing me stop outside the house, Orlaith wonders what we are supposed to do next. <Should I woof at the door?>

"No, but let's knock and go inside to see if it's been maintained."

No one answers to my knock or my call. The door is unlocked, however, and we enter cautiously. There is no electricity but I find a candelabra and a box of matches resting next to it on a parlor table and light it up.

"Do you smell anyone inside? Hear anyone?" I ask Orlaith.

<I don't think anyone is here now,> she replies. <Upstairs maybe.>

"Let me know if you hear or smell anything interesting, then. We'll check the ground floor first."

The house still looks as Fjalar had left it; wood-paneled walls with shields and crossed axes mounted on the walls. In the living room, which modern people would use as a place to retire after meals, Fjalar had placed a long wooden table with benches so that people could sit near the hearth as they ate and then remain for skalds and legends afterward. At the end of the table nearest the hearth, a yellow legal pad that does not belong there demands my attention. Stiff capital letters spell out a message: Build fire for Frigg and speak your true name to greet her.

That would work. As a healer, Frigg might actually be a better person to talk to than Odin. I don't know if this message is intended for me or for Atticus, but it appears that they anticipated our need.

"Looks like we get to build a fire," I say.

<Yay! Warm, cozy naps!>

Using wood stored in a box next to the hearth, I lay a fire and light it, waiting until it's crackling along before speaking.

"Frigg, it is Granuaile MacTiernan who calls. I have an urgent matter to discuss with you regarding Loki. Please visit me here in Colorado." I repeat this two more times and hope that's sufficient.

<Now do we go to sleep?>

"No, we go outside to the front porch. If Frigg wants to talk to me, she will arrive on the Bifrost."

And Frigg does indeed wish to talk. The rainbow bridge shimmers before us, sloping out of the northern sky to dissipate into the carpet of leaves in front of the house, and the goddess floats down, dressed in blue and white with her hair gathered in a series of braids behind her.

"Frigg, thank you for coming."

"Well met, Granuaile MacTiernan. What news regarding Loki?"

"Were you and Odin aware of his mark?"

The goddess's brows draw together. "What mark?"

I show her my arm and explain how it came to be there and what Loki said it meant. "I imagine he has branded Hel and Jörmungandr in the same way, thereby making them invisible to Odin and others. It's why we're having trouble finding them."

After a few minutes' inspection and questions about how it feels or felt in the past, and a request for a detailed description of the chop Loki used to make it, she agrees that Odin should take a look. "It is not a normal wound, by any means. Have you the time to visit Asgard?"

"I do. I'd be grateful for the invitation. May I bring my hound?"

"Of course. You shall be my guests. Come."

There is no TSA on the Bifrost. No one questions my staff or my axe. Orlaith is at first unsure she wants to step on the rainbow bridge; to her eyes, it doesn't appear that solid, and she paws at the bottom edge a few times to reassure herself that it isn't a trick of the light. But once she is satisfied that it will hold her weight, we ascend into the sky and the Bifrost proves to work like the efficient parts of airports, the moving sidewalks where you walk and the surface also moves with you, quickening the trip. We arrive in Asgard in less than a minute of walking, passing through starscapes kissed by nebulas and feeling only the briefest flash of heat from Muspellheim and a small blast of frost from Jötunheim.

It's difficult to act like this is all normal for me, but I firmly smoosh my desire to take a selfie in Asgard, because I know how deeply uncool that would be. Frigg leads me to the great hall called Gladsheim and shepherds me through a maze of passages until we arrive at Odin's throne. The throne room is almost deserted, defying my expectations. But I discover that Odin is not truly holding court at the moment. Flanked by two scowling Valkyries and a couple of wolves at his feet, Odin's single eye bores into me and I feel naked before him—not that he regards me lasciviously, but rather in the sense that I cannot hide anything from him.

His ravens are absent and with them the majority of his consciousness, so Frigg urges him to call them home. "You will need all your faculties," she tells him, "and we will need privacy for this news. Meet us in my parlor at your earliest convenience."

He grunts and we depart without me saying a word to him, and I understand that this is by design. Loki could have spies in Gladsheim.

Frigg leads me to a room decorated in bronze and ivory. We sit upon a divan together, I set my weapons aside, and Orlaith folds herself around my feet as a helmeted Valkyrie brings us a wide bowl of fruit. I take a fuzzy peach because I want to make a T-shirt saying "I dared to eat a peach in Asgard" and have it be true.

"He will not be long," Frigg assures me, and I nod, biting into one of the most glorious peaches I have ever tasted. J. Alfred Prufrock definitely should have dared.

Odin enters as I'm finishing with Hugin and Munin perched on his shoulders, all three of them alert and focusing their gaze on me.

"Granuaile," he says, nodding once by way of greeting. "We have not formally met before now."

As I stand to greet him, I'm not sure what to do with the remainders of my peach. There is no protocol that I know of that deals with how to surreptitiously dispose of fruit in the presence of a god. "I'm honored, Odin, if slightly embarrassed to be caught eating."

He grins gracefully. "The honor is mine. And not to worry." A Valkyrie appears at my elbow and takes the remainder from me, leaving my hands free. Odin thanks her and then his eye shifts down to my left arm. The beaks of his ravens tilt in tandem. "Please show me Loki's mark and explain to me precisely how it was made and what he said about it."

I lift my arm and Odin cups it in his callused hand, peering closely at the mark as I recount how Loki lured me into a forgotten room buried in India to procure the Lost Arrows of Vayu, enchanted weapons that would fly true and pierce their intended target no matter the ambient weather conditions, much like Odin's spear, Gungnir. And once I was rendered immobile by a creature guarding the arrows, Loki branded me with a round, runed chop he carried with him, from which I had been unable to heal.

The bearded god spends several silent minutes examining the mark from several angles and pressing the skin with a thick finger. Finally satisfied, he drops my arm and meets my eyes with his single one.

"I have a plan," Odin said.

"I'm very glad to hear it. This should be good."

s a Druid, I can bind myself to the mind of a creature and calm it if it is feeling aggressive or fearful. If sufficiently worried and I feel like bothering, I can also ask the elemental to prevent animals from attacking me, which Oberon calls "cheating." But if I'm going to hunt, I'm on my own. I can't ask an animal to lie down and die for me, and the rules are clear from Gaia: No magic may be used to take another creature's life. I have to do that on my own.

One of the lookout hartebeests saw us coming and bleated a warning to the herd. They sprang into flight and the ground thundered with the collective drumbeat of their hooves.

Oberon and I stayed close together at first; we had to split off a chunk of the herd that had a kid in it. We positioned ourselves to the right of center behind the herd and Oberon barked. It didn't take many before the animals directly in front of him tried to turn one way or the other, and their efforts pushed others, and in moments, we had a widening schism.

We followed the right-hand group and then we had to split up on either side of it, a dangerous game of turning the herd this way and that until the kids they were protecting in the middle eventually snapped out of the end like a whip tail. Oberon leapt onto the back of one and brought it down, the herd kept moving, and then the hunt changed into a protect-the-flag operation.

High-pitched chattering announced the approach of a pack of hyenas. It took me a moment to orient myself and figure out where we had left Mekera, but once I spotted her in the distance, I shape-shifted back to human and drew Fragarach from its scabbard. I waved it overhead, hoping the sunlight would flash on the blade and signal that she should come down.

Speaking through my bond to the earth, I asked the elemental to redirect the attention of the hyena pack elsewhere in a live-and-let-live arrangement. There had been enough blood shed for my divination already. The hyenas kept coming, though, fanning out to surround and harry us because that was how they operated, lacking the speed to chase down many animals themselves. I thought I was going to have to cut a few of them and risk Oberon getting hurt, but just as one lunged toward me, armed with teeth and hyena death-breath, it abruptly changed its mind, backed off, and then the entire pack skirted us and trotted away after the herd. I sighed in relief and Mekera arrived with my clothes shortly thereafter, untroubled. It was only an hour and a half after we took off through the grass that we returned to Mekera's house with everything she needed, and she had her cheese started before noon. Normally, separating the rennet from the stomach lining takes days or even weeks, but I sped that process along with some careful binding.

Below her living area and another level for her private suite, Mekera had a lab for bacteria cultures, a mixing room, and shelves for aging completed wheels of cheese. All of these were additions I'd made in the nineties.

Oberon was awed by the variety of cheeses on display in the aging room. <Can we take a nibble out of those?>

You just ate, Oberon, back on the savanna.

<I didn't say I was hungry. I just want to know if I'm allowed to take a bite later because they smell good.>

No, those are off-limits. We're not here to eat cheese. We're here to make cheese.

While Mekera heated the milk and watched the temperature gauge, I found a chair by the wall and sat down, staying out of her way, and Oberon lay down beside me. <Oh, yeah! She's making a magic blood cheese, right?>

Sort of. Do you want me to explain it or just say it's magic and leave it at that?

<You might as well tell me. It looks like she will be busy for a while.>

All right. Divination works to some extent because our world is a system with certain predictable constants built in like clockwork. Creatures act according to their desires and most of those desires are somehow related to hunger or sex.

<Yep, that sounds like me.>

I can predict that you would like a sausage or some quality time with Orlaith without the help of divination. But human behavior can get a little more complex, especially when people change their minds in reaction to other people or for no reason at all. Still, their behavior tends to follow patterns, and those patterns can be predicted with a fair degree of accuracy if you have the right medium and the ability to interpret it.

<And cheese is the right medium?>

It is for Mekera. I could never do what she does.

<Never?>

I suppose I could learn, but I wouldn't want to. It took her years, and I have already spent years learning other methods. Plus, look at the setup she needs to practice her art. It's a lot of equipment and you need the proper ingredients.

<So, why do it that way at all?>

Because she gets much better results than I ever could with my wands or with augury. I mean, she told me fifty years ahead of time that Tempe would be a great place to hide for about ten years starting in the late nineties. I was supposed to come back to see her after that but never did until now. Everything she's ever predicted for me has been spot-on, though—she's as close to infallible as you can get.

<But how? It's just cheese.>

No, it's pattern recognition. She watches the cheese as it transforms from one state of being to another, spurred by a natural catalyst. The pattern of the milk or cream as it curdles mirrors the pattern of the future transforming in response to the catalyst of the question she holds in her mind during the divination. The patterns created in the process of curdling the milk are almost fractal in their complexity, allowing her to see far more than anything I could manage with the juxtaposition of five wands tossed in the air.

<Hey, fractals! I remember you telling me about those. They're math things that have to do with math.>

Your memory is very impressive, Oberon.

<I know. So, what's the question you asked her?>

I haven't actually asked her yet. When she's ready, she will say so.

I was hoping she would be ready soon. Most cheeses took days to complete, and if we had the time, I would have asked for one of those, but we were doing something simple and fast because we had a deadline of sundown looming. We still hadn't seen the vampire's thrall, but he had surely called in reinforcements and we could expect them to descend upon us a couple hours after sunset. We had to reach a tethered tree well in advance of that, and there weren't any nearby.

Mekera cranked a timer and its rapid clicking as it counted down signaled to me that she was available to talk for a few minutes. Too late, she realized the same thing. Her eyes darted to me, panic around the pupils, and I spoke up before she could pretend to be busy with something else.

"Hey, let's talk about something fascinating, like why you've been living here all alone since the end of World War II."

Mekera cursed. "I *knew* you were going to bring that up."

"Have you ever talked about it with anyone? You've had more than seven decades to brood about whatever you're dwelling on."

"I find solitude therapeutic."

"Excellent. You've had lots of therapy, then, and should be able to discuss it freely."

"No."

"Help me understand, Mekera. I know we don't see each other often, but we've known each other for a long time. We met in Bahir Dar and you introduced me to coffee. Back then, you liked people. What happened?"

I got stony silence and a glower for a while, but I returned her look with patient expectation. She finally shifted her chair around so that the back faced me and she straddled it like that, hugging the frame with her arms and resting her chin on the top of it. Her eyes fell from my face and she stared at a spot on the floor, but I know that's not what she was seeing; she was visiting a memory. Her mouth drooped at the corners, then her lip quivered a bit and her eyes filled. The left one ran over and a tear trailed down her cheek.

"I lost somebody I loved," she whispered. "I know that doesn't make me special. Happens to everyone. She made me feel special, though, more than anyone else I'd met in five hundred years." She wiped at the tear on her cheek. "I don't know if we would have made it last forever, but damn if we weren't going to try."

"I'm very sorry," I replied, and didn't ask for any further details. None were necessary. Lost loved ones could be crippling sometimes.

Silence stretched out between us—apart from the ratchet noises made by the timer and Oberon's occasional snore. Like most dogs, he had the ability to nap at will.

"You had a wife back then," she said, no longer whispering but keeping her voice low. "Down in Tanzania? Married for a long time, lots of kids?"

"Yeah."

"What was her name?"

"Tahirah."

"That's right. I remember it rhymed with mine. What happened to the kids?"

"I don't know. They were all adults when I lost her, and I said goodbye and took off. Kind of like what you're doing, except I didn't isolate myself. I just went elsewhere to try to heal, try to forget. Funny thing is, I was on my way to try to reconnect with my family when I met you."

"And did you?"

"In a manner of speaking. It was a couple hundred years after I left, so I was really trying to track down descendants, and was only partially successful."

Her voice rose with irritation. "A couple hundred years? And you're giving me grief for seventy or eighty?"

"Yes, because I pulled out of it by living in the world. The kind of funk you're in doesn't appear to have an exit strategy except the final kind."

That stung her and she sat up and back, letting go of the sides of the chair and instead resting her arms on the top where her chin had been, locking the elbows and letting her hands dangle in the air. One of them twitched in my direction and her tone was brisk, impatient. "Let me ask you something, Siodhachan."

"Okay."

"Was Tahirah the love of your very long life?"

"Yes."

"Did you ever love again?"

"Yes. Rather recently, in fact. Her name is Granuaile."

"Ah, so there's hope for me!" Her mouth split into a wide but false grin. "Now, how many hundreds of years was it between Tahirah and Granuaile, exactly?"

"Come on."

"It's longer than I've been alive, isn't it?"

"Look, I'm not saying it's going to be easy and I'm not saying it'll happen at all, much less soon, but I am saying that it *is* possible to love again. Unless you're living all by yourself in the middle of a wilderness."

The timer dinged and startled Oberon awake from a dream in which he apparently had been accused of shenanigans.

<What? It's not my fault, I didn't do anything to those Chihuahuas!>

Mekera stood and made a brushing motion with her hand, waving away my concerns. "Enough. It's time to get to work. What do you want me to look for?"

I didn't think we'd reached a happy place in our conversation, but she had a point—we had to proceed since time was against us. "Well, the vampires liquidated most of my money and I kind of need it to stick it to them." Yewmen mercenaries weren't cheap. "But I can't ask you anything regarding myself or my cold iron will mess up your tyromancy."

"Do you just want money?"

"Money is my primary goal. But a close second would be some way to cause them great inconvenience and perhaps some personal grief. I don't know if personal grief is possible for vampires and lifeleeches, but a guy can hope."

Mekera stared at me unblinking for a few beats, considering, before she spoke. "I can share something with you that may sway your question," she said, "but I cannot guarantee you that it will yield anything useful."

"Please share it and I will consider carefully before asking you to proceed."

She nodded once. "Fair enough. The lifeleech did not ask me for a single cheese. He asked for two because he had two questions. One led to Kodiak Black, which you already know. The other was…strange."

"What was it?"

"He wanted to know where he could hide something from you. I remember his exact words. 'Where is the one place on earth that Siodhachan Ó Suileabháin is least likely to return?'" he asked.

"Oh, no. And you told him?"

"Yes. Toronto."

"Fuuuuck!" Toronto was the last place on earth I wanted to see again. And yet, by confessing this to me, she had made the possibility that I would return *more* likely. She could not have foreseen this pattern before, because my cold iron obscured it. My appearance there—if I chose to go—would be completely unpredictable. So, if Werner Drasche followed through on her advice, I might possibly be able to deal him some kind of debilitating blow. All I needed was the courage to return to Toronto.

Money would be simpler. Mekera could tell me where to score plenty of money fast, no problem. I could score some without her help—my abilities would make a life of crime simple if I wished. But that would hurt other people instead of Werner Drasche. And I so wanted—no, needed—to pay Werner in kind for what he did to my friend Kodiak.

"Can you tell me what he's hiding in Toronto and where?" I asked.

"Possibly. If he's hidden something there, I can tell you. But I have to warn you that he might not have acted on my advice. If I look for that answer and nothing comes up, we won't have the time to try again before sundown. You have only the one question."

"Understood," I said, and took a moment to think. I concluded that the potential payoff was too great to ignore. If it turned out to be nothing, I could pursue other methods of raising money. "Ask this: What is Werner Drasche and/or the vampire known as Theophilus hiding in Toronto and where?"

"Technically, that's not a single question," she replied, "but that should be manageable. I will ask."

"How long until sundown?" I asked, unable to tell in the depths of the basement. Mekera glanced at her wristwatch, an antique windup number on a worn leather strap.

"Three hours," she said. "Or thereabouts. I won't be able to give you anything significant for at least another hour, maybe more."

"Okay, thanks for the warning."

"You're going to have to stay awake. I report what I see as I see it and I don't repeat."

"Understood."

"Okay. Then I'll begin."

She turned back to her small industrial mixing vat, which had an automatic mixing arm spinning around in it, and poured in a beaker of rennet as the cream spun. Then she began speaking in Amharic, a musical Semitic language still spoken today, and which I did not speak. The closest language to it that I knew was Aramaic. Presumably, she was asking my question, binding it to the curdling of the milk, and catalyzing the divination.

<Do you know what she's saying, Atticus? Is it 'Lords of Kobol, bless this cheese' or something like that?>

I imagine it's something like that, but I don't know for sure.

<That's too bad. Can I go back to sleep now? I was in the middle of an exciting dream.>

I know, the one with Chihuahuas.

Oberon gave a mental snort of amusement. <Aren't they rascals?>

As Oberon drifted to sleep and Mekera continued her work, chanting and staring into the vat, I brooded on the news. I hadn't been in Toronto since 1953 and I hadn't planned on ever returning. I had chosen to go by the alias of Nigel then, which, when coupled with a tragic coincidence, turned out to be one of the worst decisions of my life. Drasche could not know the reason why, but forcing me to return there would reopen an old wound, and I could already feel my stomach churning with acid at the thought.

Shakespeare provided me solace as he so often did. In many ways, Hamlet is not a good role model, but once he's aware of his uncle's plans to have him killed in England with the aid of his erstwhile friends Rosencrantz and Guildenstern, he determines to outwit them: "And 't shall go hard, / But I will delve one yard below their mines, / And blow them at the moon."

"It's somewhere in downtown Toronto," Mekera suddenly said in English, and then amended it. "A sort of financial district." She squinted. "Do the letters R, B, and C mean anything to you?"

"Yes. That would probably be the Royal Bank of Canada."

"There you go." A pause of fifteen minutes, and then she said, "Okay, these are numbers I'm seeing related to the bank: 5, 1, 7."

"What's that for?"

"A safety deposit box is my guess. It's not long enough for a PIN number."

"All right. What's in there?"

Mekera stared at the swirling cauldron of curds for another half hour and finally shook her head, grimacing. "I can't get a grasp on any specifics. But it's not money or anything like that.

It's just…paper. A big stack of it. Information of some kind, maybe a list."

"Werner Drasche is storing a written list in a safety deposit box in the RBC and that's what he doesn't want me to find? That's what would hurt him?"

"It's both him and Theophilus. They're in this together, so that was a good call, but the answer is yes."

"Is that all?"

She pointed at the swirl of curdling milk and sighed. "It's trying to give me names and addresses, but this isn't that kind of cheese. We don't have enough time to get that specific, you understand? Because this cheese will be finished in a few minutes and it doesn't have the time to give me detailed answers, so it's rushing and it's no good. It's like when you force a high volume of water through a small area—all you get is pressure and noise."

Oberon, who I thought had been dreaming of small rascally dogs, had woken up at some point and chose to offer his own analogy. <Sounds like going to a comic con.>

You've never been to a comic con.

<No, but I've listened to you and Clever Girl complain every time you get back from one. "Gah, it was so crowded!" she always says. "The pressure! The noise!" That's a direct quote.>

"Okay, Mekera, thank you. How much time left until sundown?"

A glance at her wristwatch and she said, "A little over an hour."

"Okay, gather whatever you like and we'll run to the nearest tree I can tether."

"What about the thrall?"

"I can take care of him first if you want."

"Well, shouldn't we?"

"Not unless you believe he's an immediate threat. The vampires will be able to track us by scent whether he's alive or not. He will probably wait for the vampires to arrive and then point in whichever direction we run, hoping to be rewarded."

Mekera disagreed. "I think they will tell him to follow us and phone in updates as they close in. He has a satellite phone."

That could potentially cause problems. If we ran back toward the trees we used to shift into the area, we would be heading in the direction the vampires were most likely to come from, nearest to the local airport at Gambela. If we spent time searching for the thrall, every minute would be one less we could use in escaping. We could run away from the airport instead, searching for an exit point to the south and thus increasing the transit time of any pursuers over land, but I would then need some time to bind a new tree to Tir na nÓg. There were risks no matter what we chose.

"Do you know of a large tree somewhere to the south of here?" I asked. The small scrub species I'd seen peppering the savannah were too fragile to be anchored to Tir na nÓg.

Mekera's eyes swung up to the ceiling as she thought it over, then snapped back to me once she remembered.

"Yes. There's a baobab tree down that way, an old one."

"How far?"

The tyromancer shrugged. "Ten miles? Fifteen?"

That would probably work out well. The thrall, whoever he was, wouldn't be able to keep up with us on a ten-mile run, and the vampires wouldn't be able to move at full speed while they were tracking us.

"All right, let's go as soon as you can manage."

After consulting with Odin, the Bifrost deposits us back at the foreman's house alone. Orlaith's snout rises immediately to sample the air. <Granuaile, I smell fire. Smoke.>

Where? Not our cabin?

<Maybe. It is from that direction.>

Let's go, but quietly.

Atticus and I had warded the cabin against fire, but only the magical kind that Brighid or Loki might sling around. It's not immune to a match and lighter fluid. As we draw closer, however, Orlaith reports that the smoke isn't coming from our cabin at all. <It's down by the river,> she says.

Okay. I want to check the cabin first, though. I actually want to check the wards to see if they have been disturbed or if anyone or anything is hiding nearby. Fires are infamous distractions and I don't want to fall for it.

Putting my hand to the earth outside our cabin and speaking the words for magical sight, I examine our wards and see nothing wrong with them; they remain intact. No flames dancing in the windows, either, so that's a plus.

Staying alert and guarded, I pad down through the white pillars of aspen trees to Sneffels Creek, the cold mountain stream that eventually feeds the Uncompahgre River in Ouray, reminding Orlaith to remain at my side and not rush ahead. A plume of smoke in the air draws me to a dangerously large fire and an extremely tall figure standing over it, arms crossed.

A curtain of lank, dirty blond hair obscures his features at first, but as soon as he looks up at my approach and I see the scarred, puckered tissue around his eyes and his condescending smirk, I tell Orlaith to run back to the cabin and hide inside using the doggie door.

Go as fast as you can or he will hurt you. Don't argue; just go.

<Will he hurt you, though?>

No, he needs me for something. But he will use you to control me. If you are out of his reach, he can't control me. Go.

Orlaith turns and runs but speaks as she does. <Tell me when I can come out.>

I will.

Loki's smug grin at my approach fades as he sees Orlaith bound away.

"Aw, where's she going? We came to such a lovely understanding last time." Last time, he did something to Orlaith's mind and used her as a hostage; I wouldn't let him do that again.

"You're not welcome here, Loki. Leave."

He affects a hurt expression. "Where's your hospitality, Miss MacTiernan?"

I brandish my staff and my axe and say, "Right here. If you'd like a sample of my hospitality, say the word."

Loki's hair ignites as he scowls at me, perturbed by my attitude. "You went to Asgard."

"Indeed I did."

"Why?"

"I'm sure Odin would love to tell you all about it. He's anxious to see you, in fact. Why don't you go ask him?"

"I'm asking you."

"I'm not answering. Leave now."

The flames around Loki's head flare up and his eyes turn dark. "Perhaps you need a reminder of how this relationship works. When I need something, you get it for me, whether that be the Lost Arrows of Vayu or a simple answer to a simple question. Tell me why you went to Asgard and what you discussed with Odin," he says, and then points a finger at the cabin before adding, "or does your hound need to pay for your mouth?"

Seeing him fall back on that same threat angers me—not only because he's threatening an innocent creature but because he thinks so little of me that he doesn't think I'd have prepared for it. That's okay: He's already revealed that has a short fuse and I exactly how to set him off. "Suck my balls," I tell him.

Loki blinks. "You don't even *have*—"

"They're still bigger than yours."

He flinches as if I'd slapped him—and I suppose that, verbally, I had. Not only had I cast aspersions on his manly man-bits but I'd interrupted him to do it.

"Bitch," he growls, immediately grasping for the world that most men do when they encounter a woman they can't control. His entire body ignites into a pillar of flame and his voice snarls out of it, "It seems you need a lesson."

He rockets straight up in a ball of fire and then arcs over my head toward the cabin. *You're inside now, right, Orlaith?*

<Yes.>

Good. Stay there and don't come out, no matter what you hear.

While Loki's eyes are off me, I trigger invisibility using the bindings carved into Scáthmhaide and jog uphill, craning my neck to follow his progress. I'm curious as to how precisely the wards will affect him when he hits them, and I murmur bindings to increase my strength and speed.

When Loki hits the Druidic wards against fire, he doesn't smash against them like a bird hitting a window, which I was kind of hoping for. Instead, his fire is simply snuffed out like a candle wick between fingers, and he keeps going on inertia, a thin smoking body that's now falling out of the sky instead of flying through it. His initial cry of surprise is followed by a cry of terror as he realizes he won't be able to control his landing, and I shift from a jog to a full sprint, closing on where he'll land.

He breaks his right arm trying to cushion his fall, a sharp crack and then a wounded howl as he rolls in front of our cabin. He cradles it with his left arm for a couple of revolutions and then, as he struggles to push himself to his feet with his one good arm, I leap onto his back and sink my axe into it until the blade disappears. It's buried in his left shoulder blade and I leave it there, jumping off as he rears back and screams anew.

"Now here's a lesson for *you,* Loki: You fucked with the wrong Druid."

The god of mischief staggers to his feet and whirls around, trying to locate me, his arms dangling like useless vines. I can see him trying to reignite, little puffs of smoke popping out all around him. He won't be able to spark up until he's outside the circumference of the ward, and he shouts, "Where are—" before the edge of Scáthmhaide smashes into his teeth from his left, sending a fine collection of them spraying to the right in a mist of blood.

"Shut up," I say, twirling my staff and jabbing up into his diaphragm to drive all the air out of his lungs. "You arrange matters so that I have to watch my father get killed, lure me into a pit to get all my bones broken by some monster, and then while I'm helpless, you brand me like I fucking *belong* to you?"

Loki takes a wheezing breath and looks like he wants to answer, so I tee off on his ribs and crack a few.

"I've been trying to figure out how to get rid of your mark, and it occurred to me that the simplest thing to do would be to get rid of *you*." The mask of pain on Loki's face shifts to fear as he realizes that there's no bottom to the deep pool of shit he's stepped in. "And it's not really a selfish revenge thing on my part. It's kind of a public service, right? Because you admitted to me that you want to wipe out everything on Midgard and start over. Well, as a Druid of Gaia, I take issue with that. I am duty-bound to make sure it doesn't happen, in fact. And so, for crimes you have already committed and greater crimes you intend to commit, Loki Firestarter, your life is forfeit. I judge you guilty and sentence you to death."

Bleeding and gasping for breath, eyes wide and unfocused, Loki backs away from my voice and stumbles over a bush, startling a hare that sprints away. He tumbles backward and I charge forward, whipping Scáthmhaide down in a punishing arc at his face, but the end of my staff whiffs through his head and pounds the earth instead. His body dissolves into vapor and I look up to locate the hare, realizing he duped me with an illusion. I find it still running straight away, an uncommonly slow hare, its fur puffing and popping with attempts to ignite until finally it escapes the circle of our wards and blooms into flame. Loki's shape forms briefly, still mangled and with my axe in his back, though now the wooden handle's on fire. He glares in my general direction but says nothing—probably can't with his jaw broken. Since he can't locate me precisely and is probably worried about being taken down again, he launches himself into the sky and passes beyond my reach.

At first, I'm annoyed with myself because I should have thought to bind him to the earth right away to prevent his escape, or at least triggered magical sight so he couldn't pull a fake like that. But then I grin and laugh out loud because it felt good to get a measure of vengeance and show Loki he is not invincible; I had not expected to be so successful. Retracing my steps and examining the ground for blood, I find a handful of Loki's teeth and scoop them up. I scan the canopy of surrounding trees, and it isn't long before I spy Hugin and Munin staring back at me from an aspen. I hold up the teeth in triumph.

"Not bad, eh, Odin? We have him now."

One of the ravens croaks a response but I don't speak *corvidae.*

"Hold on, I'll make a box for them." Using the same binding principles I had used earlier to make targets for my hawk practice, I fashion a small wooden cube out of some reformed branches, drop the teeth in, and then I grab a few blood-splattered leaves and add them before sealing it up. "Ready to hop on the Bifrost." An affirmative croak, and the ravens leap off the branch and flap out of sight, returning to Odin.

Orlaith, you can come out now, but come straight to me. I don't want her straying outside the wards in case Loki decides to come back.

<Yay!> She comes bounding out of the house, tail sawing the air, and I kneel to give her a hug.

"We're going to go back to Asgard now and stay a while."

<Why?>

"Odin might be able to get rid of Loki's mark for me, and then we can go wherever we want without having to worry about him showing up."

<What about Oberon and Atticus?>

"I will let the elemental know where we are and she will tell Atticus when he gets back. He will understand and explain to Oberon. Once we are back on this plane, we can live wherever we want except here. Is there someplace you'd like to go?"

<I don't know places. But I like trees.>

"Good. Because we were thinking of a place kind of like this one in Oregon." Atticus had already told his attorney, Hal Hauk, to find a suitable place near or in the Willamette Valley.

I return to the creek and hastily shove some dirt over Loki's fire to extinguish it, tell the elemental where I'm going, and soon afterward, the Bifrost shimmers before me, inviting me to Asgard. Loki will know where I've gone and might put together that I've taken his teeth to Odin, but let him. He will know that my death sentence is tacitly approved by Odin. And he'll have to start Ragnarok now if he wants to get his teeth back, and Odin is clearly prepared to take that risk.

On my previous visit, the one-eyed god determined that Loki's mark operates much like the cold iron bound to Atticus's aura. It isn't really a thing but rather a proxy of a thing—a proxy of Loki himself, bound with a genetic key. As such, Gaia doesn't recognize it as a wound to be healed, for it is something I wear like clothes—except I can't take it off without Loki's help. The solution, Odin told me, was to kill Loki if I could—plan A, which would set Hel off for sure but forestall other plans Loki might have in motion—or go to plan B, which was to get some of Loki's genetic material to use in crafting a countermark. Blood and teeth should serve very well.

There is a lightness to my step as I walk on the Bifrost again. Loki may have gotten the better of me in India, but I had certainly gotten the better of him in Colorado, and that did much to heal the humiliation I suffered there, especially the knowledge that he'll never be able to smile about his victory again.

I am under no illusions about what this means: I am as much under Loki's death sentence now as he is under mine. But that means there will be no more games, and I am content with that. A couple lines from Whitman's *Leaves of Grass* come to mind, which in their original context have absolutely nothing to do with my situation but nevertheless seem appropriate now: *I will therefore let flame from me the burning fires that were threatening to consume me.*

Yeah. That works.

e did five-minute miles to reach the baobab tree thanks to some assistance from Gaia, but we didn't get to it until after dark because it was closer to fifteen miles than ten and Mekera took some time gathering her essentials and wrapping them up for a hard run. It turned out to be too much time.

Tethering a new tree is not an instantaneous process. It's a secure path between our plane and Tir na nÓg, after all, and even though it may take only fifteen minutes if executed perfectly, you have to have fifteen minutes free of distractions. If you interrupt the binding, then you have to start over from the beginning. Using a different headspace to deal with verbal distractions usually works, but sometimes, especially in nature, you have to worry about other things. I've had bees, for example, try to pollinate my nostril or ear because my red hair attracts them like a cluster of flowers, and once I get six legs and a pair of wings buzzing around in there, I forget about what I'm doing in all of my headspaces and just freak out. Facebees are the worst.

I learned to ask the elemental to keep other animals from bothering me after that happened a couple of times. Well, that and the constrictor that tried to slither up my pants that one time in Panama—literal trouser snakes are primally frightening.

Before I began, I told Oberon and Mekera to try to keep conversation to a minimum and took the trouble to camouflage us all to throw off the thrall, presuming he was still trailing behind us somewhere. I also gave us all night vision before contacting the elemental, asking for a short span of time free of insects and predators around the baobab tree. That done, I divided my consciousness between my Old Irish headspace for the tethering and English for everything else, and informed my companions that I was beginning. In fifteen minutes, we'd be able to shift away to Tir na nÓg, and from there, we could shift again to Emhain Ablach, where Mekera would have her safety and solitude.

Apart from a knapsack of clothes and some bubble-wrapped vials of bacteria cultures and vegetable rennet for her future work, she had brought her bow and quiver along with a wheel of hard cheese she said was precious to her. I assumed it was the stuff she ate to prolong her life; she had already been a couple hundred years old when I met her in the sixteenth century. The rest of her cheese she had to abandon, and this triggered Oberon's sympathy so much that he spent much of the run trying to compose the "Abandoned Cheese Bleus." I would give him a snack later for the pun.

Mekera had occasion to pull out her bow about four or five minutes later when the thrall showed up, proving that he not only existed but that he possessed extraordinary stamina. A slim man built for long-distance running, he had the satellite phone she'd spoken of to his ear, and he was speaking into it as he approached. The vampires had equipped him well; he was wearing night vision goggles. If they were the kind that amplified and enhanced ambient light and the lower end of infrared spectrum they wouldn't let him see through our camouflage. If they were thermal imagers, however, he'd spot us. The camouflage binding did nothing to disguise our body heat, and that's how a sniper was able to target me once in Germany.

Without discussing it with me, I heard Mekera draw an arrow from her quiver, nock it on her bowstring, and shoot the thrall in the chest as he slowed to a walk near the tree, searching for us—he clearly didn't have the thermal imaging. He squawked as he went down, and I broke off her camouflage because I wanted to see what she was doing. She ran out to finish him off if he needed finishing, dropping her bow and yanking out her hunting knife. I saw her dip out of sight in the grass for a couple of seconds, but she rose again with the sat phone up to her ear, speaking loudly enough that I could hear her. The connection was still open, and evidently, the thrall offered no resistance to her taking the phone.

"You're too late," she said. "We killed your thrall and we're shifting out of here now. Tell Drasche I said his clothing is about as attractive as a festering baboon's ass." She listened for a few seconds and then disconnected with a thumb before tossing the phone into the grass.

I couldn't say much because I had to keep speaking the words of the binding in Old Irish, but I dropped my camouflage too, and my face must have communicated a challenge to Mekera when she returned.

"What? I told you I have a strict no-stalking policy."

"Noted," I said, when I could find a pause in the phrases of the binding to slip in an English word.

"Anyway, they're going to be here soon. As in a few minutes. As in before you finish whatever you're doing. Don't know how many, though."

Even one was too many. There was no way that Mekera or Oberon could stand up to a vampire. She might be able to surprise one with an arrow to the heart; I noticed that she had wooden shafts, expertly fletched, and those would serve if she could get in a lucky shot, but she wouldn't get more than one.

I couldn't imagine that there would have been time to gather a large number of vampires here so quickly after sundown. We could be looking at two or three, no more—the surrounding population wouldn't support any more. These had to have come from Gambela itself or perhaps Gore to the east. More would be coming in, though, if they thought they could delay me—and they could. They already had, because I couldn't ignore them. My best option would be to deal with them as quickly as possible and then begin the tethering again, hoping that no more vampires showed up in the interim. Sighing in frustration, I halted the binding and stood, slapping at my jeans to get the dust off them.

"I'd like you and Oberon behind the tree," I said to Mekera. The trunk was easily wide enough to conceal them both.

"They'll know we're there."

"I know, but they're after me anyway and I want their eyes on the prize."

<Atticus, I want to help.>

I know, buddy, but these guys are really fast and strong. If you try to fight them, you'll get hurt, no doubt about it, and I don't want that.

<But you could get hurt too.>

I'll do my best not to.

They turned out not to be guys. The vampires were two women in loose-fitting robes that streamed behind them as they ran. But unlike the vampire that had ambushed us in close quarters, these two were far enough away that they could be dispatched easily. I triggered my charm of unbinding repeatedly as they approached, using it as a range-finding exercise. When it finally hit them about a hundred yards away, they both clutched their chests and did a faceplant. That allowed me time to unbind one of them, and once that was done, I made a macro out of it, changed the target, and unbound the other without ever having to draw my sword.

Yes, the ancient vampire Theophilus had good reason to fear Druids. And had he left me alone and not declared that he wished to wipe us out for good, I wouldn't be terminating all of his minions in an effort to get to him. My little mercenary scheme with the yewmen had only begun to balance the scales he tipped in the vampires' favor long ago, and I had a long way to go before those scales were even, much less tilting in my favor. If those names and addresses locked up in a Canadian bank were of the vampire leadership—an offline, secure location for crucial information—then I could use them to wreak significant havoc. Especially if they included the whereabouts of Theophilus himself.

"All right, you two," I said, "let's reset the clock. Camouflage back on. Fifteen minutes to departure. Let me know if you hear or smell any more coming."

Fourteen of those minutes were gloriously worry-free. Insects buzzed but didn't buzz too closely to any of my orifices. Vultures figured out something had died nearby and were circling above the body of the thrall, a bit uncertain about our designs on it. And then a distant growl began, something unnatural that gradually became a motor.

<Someone's driving toward us in a Jeep, Atticus,> Oberon said. <Where they're going they don't need roads. Maybe it's Dr. Emmett Brown?>

Mekera confirmed the Jeep sighting a moment later, and then its headlights stabbed into the darkness, leaving no doubt. I kept going with the binding, though, hoping we'd have enough time to slip away. The fact that they were coming in a Jeep rather than on foot suggested someone on board was not a vampire. More thralls, perhaps. Or it could conceivably be Werner Drasche in person. If that thrall had called us in at dawn, Drasche would have had time to fly here from most places in Europe.

Oberon, get next to the tree now. We'll be shifting before that Jeep gets here. Aloud, in between Old Irish phrases, I said to Mekera, "Get your stuff. Touch the tree. We're shifting."

I didn't see her do it since we were all in camouflage, but I heard Mekera shoulder her quiver and knapsack as the rumble of the Jeep grew louder and the lights grew brighter, shuddering as the suspension tried to deal with the uneven surface of the plain. I finished tying up the knots of the tether to Tír na nÓg just as the Jeep reached about sixty or so yards away; they were probably tracking the thrall's satellite phone.

Counting on the darkness and my camouflage to keep me invisible and on their engine to mask the sound of my movement, I scrambled to my feet and laid hands on the tree, then had to drop my camouflage so that Mekera and Oberon could find me. They needed physical contact both with me and with the tethered tree to shift.

And in the time it took for them to spot me and move, I was visible to the occupants of the Jeep. I didn't know how many were there—I couldn't see past the glare of the headlights—but one of them was definitely Werner Drasche.

"O'Sullivan!" he barked in his Austrian accent, and then he shot me. Or rather, he shot the tree three times, and shot me once. He wasn't a very good marksman in a moving vehicle and he was clearly aiming for my head. Tree bark exploded above me and then a slug punched into my back, midway down and to the left, making a hash of my spleen. It didn't pass through, which meant I had to shift with it—and that was fine. The exit wound would have left blood behind for him to play with, and if I stayed around any longer I might have more serious wounds—or a wounded hound or tyromancer.

Oberon and Mekera both yelped and I felt a tug on my amulet as I shifted us to Tir na nÓg, a familiar tug that meant the lifeleech was trying to drain my energy—and that of my companions. I felt the tether snap behind us as we arrived near the edge of the Fae Court, which meant Drasche had tried to prevent my escape by killing the baobab tree.

He had apparently targeted the area around it, since Oberon and Mekera had also been hit. The two of them swayed on their feet, dizzy and weak, and I knelt beside them, drawing energy through the strained connection to earth and feeding it to them, ignoring my spleen for the moment.

<Atticus, I feel tired all of a sudden.>

I'm trying to fix that.

"What hit us?" Mekera asked, holding a hand to her head.

"The crazy ascot-wearing fool. He took a sip of your energy. He would have taken more if we had stayed there. I'm giving you some back, but you should be fine with some calories and rest."

"It was weird. I felt a sharp pain all over, and then it was as if I'd fallen into a comfy chair and didn't have the strength to get out of it. Like a blood donation where they take a bit too much. The sting of the needle and then your life gets siphoned away. Hey, you have a hole in your back."

<What? Atticus, you're hurt?>

"Yeah. I'll see to it in a minute," I said, answering them both. "Are you two feeling a little bit better?"

"I'm still tired but not dizzy anymore."

<Same here.>

"Good." The pain from my gunshot wound was beginning to assert itself and I shut it off. It was time to remove the bullet. "Mekera, would you mind holding your palm about a foot over the hole?"

"What for?"

"I need you to catch the bullet."

"Excuse me?"

"I'm just going to bind the bullet inside me to your palm, and that way, I can start healing."

"Bind it, like, permanently?"

"No, only for a moment." After the slug wriggled out of me and flew to Mekera's hand, I triggered my healing charm and let my body start dealing with the damage. It would be best to take a day or two to rest, and Emhain Ablach would be a lovely place to do that, but I had an advantage now and I didn't want to waste it. I knew precisely where Werner Drasche was and it was a hell of a long way from Toronto.

He'd left a note with Kodiak Black's girlfriend that said to find him because we needed to talk, but he'd just proven he'd rather shoot me than talk to me. We were on the same page, then.

Drasche knew I'd spoken to Mekera, because the thrall had told him. He would have had all day to call someone in Toronto and I could have a party waiting for me there. Or he might have been so eager to catch me that he didn't think of it—or he believed Mekera when she told him I'd never go back there.

Who could be waiting for me in Toronto? Besides Drasche, only Theophilus himself would give me any trouble—that or a whole lot of vampires. But they'd hardly be out during the day, and it wasn't likely that anyone else besides Theophilus or Drasche would have the key to the safety deposit box. The faster I moved, the more likely I'd score whatever was there to score; I could let my spleen heal on the way. But first, Mekera needed to get out of Tír na nÓg. A couple of faeries had dipped down to investigate who had arrived, saw that it was the Iron Druid, and flittered away again. More would come eventually, and it wouldn't be long before some liveried official of the Court inquired on Brighid's behalf what I was doing there.

"All right, let's get you to Emhain Ablach."

Gathering around a tethered tree, we shifted to the Isle of Apples, a sort of paradise for Manannan Mac Lir's horses and I suppose pie aficionados and cider heads. I know that Goibhniu used to harvest a few bushels every year and make a limited-press hard cider for Beltane.

Always fragrant and blessed with a sort of eternal summer like Tír na nÓg, it wasn't difficult to see why Manannan used it to relax.

Mekera's face, skeptical at first, eased and brightened after a few seconds of looking around and taking in a couple of deep breaths. "You weren't lying," she said.

"Well…no." I didn't have the energy to be offended.

"Did you tell me everything, though? Who else will be here?"

"As I said before, Manannan Mac Lir, god of the sea, will visit from time to time. I'll let him know you're here and he can bring you whatever you need. You'll have horses, birds, and bees around. No real living space, but lots of apples to eat."

"I'm not worried about shelter. Looks like it's mild here." She waved a finger at the canopy of apple trees all around us. "Are these all the same?"

"No, they're bunched in different varieties. You'll see and taste differences as you walk around."

<Does he have Oxheart Pippin apples here? Or Smokey Mountain Limbertwigs?>

Oberon…what?

<They're what all the hipster apple snobs are eating, Atticus. Show me a bearded man pretentiously wearing thrift store clothing, and I'll show you a dude eating a Smokey Mountain Limbertwig he waited to fall naturally into the bird nest on top of his head. I saw a whole program on heirloom fruits, and they couldn't shut up about these apple varieties.>

I'm not sure Manannan has heard of them if they're a North American thing, but I'm sure that whatever he has here is delicious.

Mekera nodded to herself in satisfaction and shifted her knapsack of goodies from one shoulder to the other. "I think I'll take that walk around. You have time to come with?" Her eyes flicked down to my back. "If you're feeling up to it?"

"I should be going—" I began, and Oberon interrupted me.

<Aw, come on, Atticus, please? Just a short walk?>

"—But I suppose I could accompany you for a while."

"Good. We're allowed to sample the fruit? It's not forbidden?"

"All you want. No forbidden fruit here."

She plucked two from the nearest branch, their skins a pale rose shot through with streaks of yellow, and tossed me one of them. "You first," she said.

I chose to be amused rather than annoyed that she suspected I'd brought her to an island full of poisoned apples. I tore into mine without hesitation and it was delightful, crunchy and sweet with just a tiny hint of tartness. Seeing that, she took a bite of hers. "Damn, that's tasty," she said around a mouthful. I nodded agreement, and we began walking.

All right, Oberon, why do you want to stay here so badly?

<I've been thinking about recipes for *The Book of Five Meats*, Atticus, and if we're going to write the definitive work on the subject, we have to start with quality ingredients. I figure this god-tended grove will give me the best apples in the universe for my chicken apple sausage.>

Do you see my eyes rolling at you right now?

<My chicken apple sausage recipe will change the world!>

Apples are only one ingredient. Where do you expect to get the finest chicken for this?

<Well, remember how Brave Sir Robin nearly fought the Vicious Chicken of Bristol? We need to go there and fight that vicious chicken and make sausage out of her.>

Oberon, that's not a real chicken. Monty Python made that up.

<Legends are always based in truth, Atticus! You taught me that! If we go to Bristol, I bet we will find a vicious chicken. The viciousness will add to its deliciousness.>

You're going to lose interest in this as soon as I give you another bath.

<No, I won't! This is a thing for us to do together. Our masterpiece. What's the point of fighting for your friends' lives and stuff if you don't live your life with them?>

He had a point. *Okay, taste test incoming.* I plucked an apple for him and lobbed it in his direction. He snatched it out of the air and began his awkward chewing.

<Oh, yeah, this will do nicely, Atticus. My recipe for Vicious Chicken Apple Sausage is going to be so very succulent. Can we raid the henhouse next?>

I'm sorry, buddy, we have to go to Toronto after a quick stop at the cabin.

<Okay, but promise we'll go to Bristol soon?>

As soon as we can.

"Mm," Mekera said, finishing her apple and tossing the core. "So—just to review—who knows I'm here?"

"Just me, and soon, Manannan Mac Lir. It's like a paradise made of privacy and vitamin C. But look, Mekera—"

The tyromancer affected a look of concern. "You said you should be going, right?"

"Ah. I'm trampling on your solitude already?"

She beamed at me, pleased I had figured it out so quickly. I think that once she saw me confirm the apples were safe, she was ready for me to go, and had endured me just long enough to finish. "Thanks for the walk. See you when you've rid the world of vampires, Siodhachan."

"May harmony find you, Mekera." I sincerely hoped it would.

"You know what?" A slow smile spread on her face as she looked around her. "It might. I'm grateful to you for the talk. I'm not ready to deal with the world's cruelties yet, but I'm willing to think about it now."

"Good enough."

Oberon and I shifted to our cabin in Colorado, where someone had left a once-sizeable fire burning down by the creek and then smothered it with a layer of dirt. Granuaile and Orlaith were nowhere to be found, but the elemental informed me they were in Asgard in the company of Odin, trying to remove Loki's mark.

"Well, I guess I can't avoid it any longer, Oberon," I said, after showering and changing into something that wasn't caked with mud. "I have to go back to Toronto as Nigel."

<I thought you said you never want to be Nigel in Toronto.>

"You don't. But I don't want a protracted war either, and being Nigel for a while is the best way I can think of to keep it short."

<So, we're at war? I'm going to knock a squirrel out of a tree in Toronto and bark at him: "This! Is! Canada!">

I scratched my friend behind the ears. "That's all the war I ever want you to see."

**To be continued in *Staked*, book 8 of the
Iron Druid Chronicles**

NOT MY CIRCUS, NOT MY MONKEYS

A Blud Novella

Delilah S. Dawson

1

I shoot my cuffs, step into the dining car, and play my favorite game: Who should I kill?

Not that I'm going to kill anyone. I'm not allowed to—and it would be bad manners. So, I just smile my sharp smile and nod my polite nods and cut through the crowd of placid humans like an elegant shark through a school of fish. They unconsciously shift and part as they wait in line for their lunch, turning away as I pass and tugging up their collars, fidgeting with their gloves. Silly creatures.

Before I've reached his window, the cook has already deposited a blood vial on the counter for me and disappeared. My fingers tighten around the still-warm glass tube, and I know who I would choose, who I would kill and drain until he was utterly empty: the vile gobbet of flesh holding court in his corner of the caravan's dining car. Barnum himself.

Kill the ringmaster, take the circus. Easy as that.

Barnum sees me watching him, and his fat finger draws a line across his well-covered throat in warning. I walk a fine line here, as the only Bludman in a company of humans, daimons, and freaks. He needs my magic, but he keeps me on a short chain, and I have a bad habit of slipping my collar. One more mark against me, and he'll either call the Coppers to drag me off to some dank city's dungeon or drain me himself and make a pretty penny bottling my forbidden but intoxicating blood. *Tit for tat*, the old duffer would say, silver coins dancing in his eyes.

With the slightest bow to my all-too-mortal master, I pocket the blood vial and leave the wagon. I'll be damned if I'm going to spend all afternoon among the caravan's human riffraff, discussing weather and the popular cut of trousers with the creatures who should rightfully be my prey. One day, I'll rule this circus, or something like it, and on that day, things will change.

Criminy's Clockwork Caravan has rather a ring to it. Much better than *Barnum's Traveling Circus*. Not that anyone can tell old Barnum that.

Back in my closet of a room in one quarter of a proper wagon, I flick the cork from the vial as easily as I could rip Barnum's head off his neck. The blood is cooler than I prefer, lumpier than blood has any right to be, and carries the taste of the sea, tangy and wild, which means it's at least two weeks old . and was taken as payment when we were camped by the shore. One copper coin or one vial of human blood: That's the only way to get through the circus turnstiles—unless you'll work for less than that. Two tubes a day is standard, but Barnum only allows me one so I'll know my place.

Hours later, just as the circus starts up for the night, I entertain myself by picking the locks on the dining wagon and pocketing half a dozen vials of blood. I think of Barnum's pulsing jugular as I drink them one after the other, swirling through the caravan's shadows in a floor-length cape as I hurry to the stage. The audience is waiting for me, so close that I can smell their excitement and fear. I wipe the red from my lips, lick the dregs from my fangs, toss the vial to the ground, and whirl out from behind the black velvet curtain in a clatter of glitter and calliope pipes.

Everyone in the crowd wants to be chosen. From the lantern-lit stage, I see a sea of eager faces and waving, gloved hands. It's rare that a human from the city can interact safely with a tame Bludman like myself, a dapper gentleman in topper and tails with a cultured accent and a smile hiding fangs. I look twenty, but I'm so much more than that. And they have no idea. They live such small lives, have such small thoughts. They think me a monster, manacled in satin and doeskin, and they're not wrong.

It's always a woman that I choose, though. The way they're trapped inside their homes, herded behind the high walls of cities, and kept far from a proper education and world view—it makes them pliant and suggestible and eager to please. They practically hypnotize themselves.

She can't be the loveliest girl in the audience, the one I select. That just makes the plainer girls jealous. But it's also hard to manufacture chemistry with a homely dullard. What I need is a pretty girl, not too slender and not too plump, not too petite and not too tall, neither a glossy blonde nor a vivacious redhead. She must be agreeable and innocent, with a certain universal girl-ness to her, a shy, dimpled maid in whose wide brown eyes all the other girls can envision themselves.

A girl I can fleece, but who'll be glad of the fleecing, you see.

That's part of the magic.

There she is. Third row, flowered bonnet, pink dress that covers her from throat to toes, wrist to wrist. Rosy cheeks, mouth open just a little in excitement to show gapped front teeth. I grin a perfect grin and whip out my arm, flinging sequins and fireflies into the air to rain down on the crowd.

"You, love."

I point at her and turn my hand over, curling my finger at her, drawing her to me. She gasps and puts a gloved hand to her well-covered chest, laughs at her good luck. Her two friends push her towards the stage, and she blushes as I hold out that same blood-red velvet glove to help her up the steps between the lights.

"What's your name, darling?" I ask as I lead her to a gilt-armed chair in the center of the stage.

"Elise. It's...Elise, sir."

"Have you ever been hypnotized, Elise?"

She sits, daintily, as if the chair might explode from too much weight. "I...no. No, sir."

I chuck her under the chin, leaving the barest swipe of pinkish powder hidden under her high, lacy collar. "Well, then. You're in for a treat."

"Will it...hurt, sir?"

A low chuckle drifts through the crowd. Do they want it to hurt? Perhaps.

I lean down to whisper in her ear and she shivers. "No, love. You won't feel a thing. Just do as I ask, and everyone will clap for you. You're the star tonight."

She nods, and I step back with a swirl of my cape. The crowd goes silent, expectant. Many of them have never seen a circus before, and no one has seen an act like mine. Some things are more real than others, and I am the former. Very few of the people on the other side of the footlights will ever understand the difference between legerdemain and true magic.

"The lovely Elise has volunteered to help us today, and for that, she will be richly rewarded. Tell me, Elise. What is your heart's dearest desire?"

Her mouth drops open as she struggles for the right answer, gloved hands shaking as they clutch the chair's arms. "To marry well and have healthy children."

Well, of course it is, you unimaginative twit. Which I don't say out loud.

"A fair request that I'm sure Saint Ermenegilda will hear and grant. And now, tell me: What is your darkest fear?"

Her eyes flash in terror and embarrassment, and she looks down at my polished boot tips, which can't help but show her the worst of herself. "Being drained," she whispers. She could mean by bludrats in the city or bludbunnies in the fields, but what she really means is me, or someone like me.

But the audience didn't hear that. They never do.

Louder, I say, "What's that, Elise? You're afraid to be turned into a chicken?"

The crowd erupts in laughter, and she splutters a bit and gives me a wobbly grin.

"But...but...BUCK BUCK BACAW!" It erupts from her rosebud mouth as she leaps up from her chair, tucks her fists into her corseted waist, and jerkily pecks her way across the stage.

Her eyes are glazed over now, the crowd is loving it, and I twist a lone feather in my fingers and continue whispering under my breath. Elise hops up onto her chair and settles down in an unladylike crouch, making the crass lads up front howl. Her clucking builds to a surprised cackle, and she stands and lifts her skirts just a little, revealing a sky-blue egg between her high, buttoned boots.

"And wake," I mutter.

"What…what happened?"

As if on cue, she swoons, and I catch her in a dramatic sweep of pink taffeta. Ever so gently, I set her atop the skull-sized egg on the chair, and it breaks with a loud crack.

"Oh!"

She stands and reaches for the pile of shards, withdrawing a simple slip of paper.

"Go on, darling," I urge. "Give it a read."

I love to watch their faces during this part, the moment they understand that magic is real. Her true love's name will be written there, possibly the names of her future children. One girl saw that her beau was sneaking out with another lass and leaped into the crowd to strike him with his own cane. But this girl does something completely new.

Elise gasps.

Faints.

Falls to the ground.

When I check her pulse, I find that she is dead.

2

---

do what any self-respecting predator would do: I pretend like it's part of the act.

"Oh, tut. Poor girl must've had rather a surprise, eh?"

They laugh nervously, then raucously. Reaching for the slip of curled paper in her hand, I study it. The handwriting is familiar; my own, of course. But the words are unlike anything I've seen before, and I've done this trick a thousand times or more.

"You have a bad heart and will die immediately of shock. The magician, if wise, will run."

I stand and shake my head. "The lad whose name is written on this slip will have his hands full with this one."

Whispers rustle, skirts sway, gloved hands curl around warm, pink ears so they won't miss my next proclamation.

"Who is it, then?" a brash fellow calls.

I just smile, careful to keep my lips over my fangs. "Wouldn't you like to know?"

With a dramatic twirl, I whip the black cape off my shoulders and drape it over the girl's still form, grateful that she's a wee thing and fits completely under the light-sucking velvet. My heart bangs around, and I quickly wipe away a drop of red-tinged sweat before the innocents in the audience grow any more fevered. I've never done this before, not with something as big as Elise.

A few mumbled words, slurry as old blood, and the cape flutters the last few inches to the ground, leaving two lumps behind. Hiding my sigh of relief, I flip it back onto my shoulders to reveal her high buttoned boots—empty, thank goodness--which I pick up and toss to the blushing boy.

"You'll find her at the candy floss machine," I say. "I imagine you two have a lot to discuss."

As the crowd stares at him in fascination, I reach deep into my pockets. Normally, I would juggle fire and breathe rainbows and produce a unicorn from my top hat. But I don't have that kind of time today. The crowd parts to let the boy with the boots past, and he's walking as if he's going somewhere horrible and can't wait to get there. I don't want to be around when he realizes she's not showing up, barefoot and laughing, by the candy floss machine. Not now and not ever. I didn't kill this girl, easy as it would've been, but no court in the land would ever find me innocent.

"Abracadabra!" I cry, flinging two fists' worth of powder into the air over the crowd.

What happens next is pandemonium, all my spells going off at once.

A glowing dragon appears in a shower of sparks, spiraling after a flurry of butterflies. Fireworks explode like giant flowers, and a troupe of dancing bludbunnies in natty jackets jigs across the stage. Eyes light up in wonder, mouths open to *ooh*, and I disappear in a puff of lavender smoke.

By the time the illusions vanish, I'm dressed in plainer clothes, carrying nothing but a grimoire and scurrying away on the moors like the prey I never thought I'd be.

3

I am Criminy Stain, and I am the master of my destiny.

The master of my destiny is currently skulking around a birch forest, watching a very attractive Bludwoman who has no business being here. She has a picnic basket over her arm, and I'm rather surprised when she pulls out a steaming teapot of blood and starts splashing it all around the clearing, painting the stark white and black trees in sprays of poppy red.

This is the height of art.

I have never been so entranced in all my life.

After a week of wandering, I'd stopped here to sleep, mainly because it was pretty, and because there was a large caravan slumbering just a few miles away. But before I could investigate it, she showed up, this marvel of a creature. Lush, auburn hair in riotous ruby curls, heavy bangs hiding green-black eyes like a bottomless pond. Swan shoulders and bloody fingers and a golden rope around her waist like a belt, the hem of her green dress dipped in mud. She scans the horizon, searching for something. I don't think it's me she's expecting, but I'm what she will get, nonetheless. I straighten my topper, check the buttons on my trousers, and prepare to step dramatically from behind a larch in a swirl of cape and magic.

"Greetings! I'm—"

"A bit creepy, actually," she finishes for me. Bored eyes flick to my face, skim up and down like she's reading a bad poem, and return to the horizon. Even her back is beautiful. "Now hush."

"Criminy Stain," I finish.

"That's rubbish. Really. Be quiet. It's almost here."

No woman has ever spoken to me like this. I'm too stunned to speak. In the embarrassed silence that follows, I hear something coming. It moves through the forest like an elephant decimating a crowd, brave and large and proudly crashing. With a fussy sigh, I slip off my gloves and tuck them into my breast pocket. My clawed fingers curl into weapons, my teeth bared as I scent the approaching beast.

"Get behind me," I say, voice low.

Her response? She flicks her fingers at me and unties the rope at her waist. Which is a little disconcerting. Ladies undressing in my presence is nothing new, but they don't usually do it when we're about to be attacked in a blood-spattered forest.

Usually.

"Let me handle this, please. I'm sure you mean well, but you're bound to muck it up." She grins coquettishly as she fiddles with her rope in the center of the clearing. "Master Stain."

I lean against the nearest unbloody tree, mimicking her lack of predation and self-preservation, and knowing that my long, dark hair and cloudy gray eyes are perfectly complimented by the background. "Would you at least do me the honor of your name before we're both attacked, love?"

"My name is Merissa," she says. "And technically, I don't believe one can be attacked when one has purposefully lured a monster in with the express purpose of capturing it."

"Capturing it?"

With a sudden spin, she kicks me neatly just above the stomach, knocking out my breath, and begins to swing her strange rope in a circle while I goggle at her. It's possibly the most helpless I've ever felt, and damned if it isn't riveting.

What the hell is she about?

In a rain of leaves and a shower of branches, a huge form barrels into the clearing, knocking over a small tree on the way. Gigantic hooves skid to a stop in the mud, and a horse the size of a volcano screams its challenge at the slight woman twirling her rope.

"Same to you," she says tartly, and tosses the rope over its great head, easy as death.

"Look, love," I wheeze, my wind barely returned. "Shouldn't you--"

"Shut up or I'll kick you again. Let a lady work."

Sure enough, she's working the horse now, taking control of it with her body and her rope. It's a white bludmare, probably the largest animal on the continent, and its back is taller than the crown of Merissa's lovely auburn head. With a tail that drags the ground, a mane that falls like rotten curtains, and a coat that should be gleaming white but is actually the color of old bone clotted with earth, the mare is magnificent and bestial and the sort of monster I would love to take in a fair fight. My instinct is to kill it myself and drink deeply, both satisfying my craving for blood and violence and, one might hope, impressing the lady.

But she's politely requested I not do that, and she seems to know her business. My understanding of horses is limited to fighting and eating them, but she's treating this one like a treasure, like possibly a friend. The mare's skin shivers over as Merissa runs hands all over it, and whenever the horse jumps away from her, she allows it, then approaches calmly again. The creature's frothing mouth is open just enough to show fangs the size of the woman's forearm, but for some strange reason, the mare's not biting her. Just putting up with her.

As she's been putting up with me.

The girl has a deft touch with beasts, is all I'm saying.

"Shh. Shh," she murmurs, and the horse snorts. "I'll call you Luca. Would you like that?" The horse shakes her head. "Picky bitch. Kali, then." The mare blows air in a satisfied sort of way, and Merissa grins at me as she rubs Kali's bloodstained nose. "You could've saved yourself a bit of trouble if you'd had the good sense to select a less ridiculous name, Mr. Stain."

"I generally kill anyone who snickers," I admit.

"You've that look about you. Now make yourself useful and put an arm over Kali's back while I knot up a halter, will you?"

And I do, because it means I can get closer to her, and because not doing so would brand me a coward.

"Let me tell you what I think, Mr. Stain. I think you're on the run from something, gadding about in the forest all alone. I can tell you're a man of taste and refinement who's not afraid to get his hands dirty. And I can also tell that you're younger than you act and older than you look. In short, sir, I do believe you are trouble and you like it that way."

She's got a tied rope harness over the horse's great nose now and nods to let me know I'm unnecessary.

I tip my hat and bow as soon as I'm out of kicking range. "What's your point, poppet?"

"You amuse me. But don't think for a moment that you'll make me swoon, sweep me off my feet, or in any other way gain the upper hand in this relationship."

"Ah, so we've a relationship now? Grand. I accept."

Taking a fistful of the horse's cobweb mane, she executes an utterly impossible leap and lands lightly on the broad, white back, making the mare jig around. The girl's so wee, I'm surprised Kali can even feel her. Perhaps it's the way her pointy little boots are lodged in the horse's ribs or how she pulls the rope halter to and fro that keeps her in charge. I do believe that I, were I underneath her, would move with rather a lot more purpose.

"Will you walk or ride?" she calls down.

I take the hand she offers. "What fool would walk when he can let someone else do all the hard work?"

With a sudden yank, she helps me swing up onto the beast's back, and unlike her, my weight is noticed. The horse's muscles bunch in annoyance, and she turns her regal head and glares at me, showing fangs.

"You'll have to share her, mate," I say, and Merissa laughs.

"She'll have to share me rather a lot. I need two of them, matched, for my act, you know."

Her body ripples against mine, and she says, "Hup, Kali!" and then we're running like hell through the forest, dodging trees as the bludmare's hooves dig divots in the leaf mould. I've never ridden like this before, but I have a good enough idea that the best way to get through such a situation involves holding on rather tightly to the ravishing if peculiar creature in front of me and not making a fool of myself. The beast has a certain rhythm that I'm quick to find, and my thighs grip her ribs and the lady's hips as my hands join around Merissa's waist. She doesn't seem to mind and lies lower over the mare's neck, her doll hands tangled in billowing white mane. When Merissa let out a great, dancing laugh, her elation travels into my veins and settles there with what feels like significant permanence.

In this moment, I am smitten and I am smote. There is no difference.

Her mostly proper updo falls mostly down, and I will know the scent of her hair forever, a mix of violets and smoke and rich, black soil. Keeping my eyes open becomes an exercise in pain as her hair whips me to tears, so I tuck my face against her shoulder and trust her to steer our mighty steed to whatever end she has planned. And why not? The thread of my former comfortable if stunted life was severed as soon as Elise died at my feet. When a man has nowhere to go, he might as well go anywhere. And if that journey can begin wrapped around the most beautiful, intriguing spitfire of a woman he's ever met, all the better.

I smell the caravan before I see or hear it. There's no mistaking the scent of last night's crowd and its sugary, salted leavings. Bits of popcorn and candy floss and sticky, fallen butterscotch apples litter the ground before a long train of wagons that's noticeably shabbier than my last home.

Merissa sits up straight and murmurs silly things to the horse, and the mare's ears flick back as she slows to a lumbering walk. Over her pretty head, I register a well-kept tightrope, brightly colored but oft-patched tents, and striped poles strung with lanterns. To my proprietary eye, it's a serviceable if untidy caravan, although at this hour of the morning, its carnivalleros would do better to be outside, practicing and performing the routines and prop maintenance that would insure many more years of good spirits.

In short, it's a place that could use my particular brand of loving cruelty, and I immediately wish to possess it, to which end I straighten my waistcoat and collar, retie my cravat, and smooth back my long hair into a tidier tail.

"Who's the master of this house, then?" I ask.

Merissa shakes her head and snorts. "Old duffer named Bartholomew Bailey. Human, fat as a maggot. Too paranoid to come out of his wagon these days after he was attacked by the wolf boy. Does business over a loudspeaker and through a tiny window, like a postal clerk. It's all a bit embarrassing, you know. But of course, there are creatures that flourish in an absence of leadership, and most of 'em have teeth." She turns her head with a practiced flip of her mad hair and gives me a sparkling smile that makes my stomach swoop in an agreeable sort of way.

"Well, love," I murmur in her ear, "have any use for an accomplished magician?"

Her shoulder lifts and falls. "We already have one. Perhaps there's a use for you in the Freak Tent, if you make a fine barker."

"Oh, I can bark. But I'd rather battle your reigning charmer and take his place."

The horse stops and sighs, and Merissa manages to slide off without touching me. When she looks up, her eyes seem to glow red. "Don't even try. He's very good. He'll rip you to shreds."

"Oh, so you know the future. Are you a fortune-teller, then?" I ask playfully.

She chuckles. "I'm a woman."

And she slaps the horse's rump, which makes Kali leap forwards with a scream, throwing me backwards. It takes every bit of cleverness I have to turn the flailing fall into a neat back flip, but I've been in the circus long enough to have trained as an acrobat. Landing neatly on my feet, I whip off my hat, bow deeply, and hold out a bouquet of blood-red roses.

"Oh, I noticed," I say with a grin.

4

She doesn't take the flowers. Doesn't point me in the direction of her grub-like Master Bailey. With steps somehow both firm and dainty and hips swaying like a cobra, she saunters to her dirty white steed, plucks her rope from the ground, and leads the now-placid creature away.

But I know this dance, and I am an old hand at legerdemain. Even without a single soul visible, I understand the workings of this circus as well as a chirurgeon knows the inside of a man's chest cavity. Stuffing the flowers back into my hat, I settle the topper firmly on my head and shoot my cuffs, heading off for the same thing the chirurgeon seeks: the object of brightest shining red.

Sure enough, painted on the side of the red wagon in elegant curlicues is *Master Bailey's Circus of Wanders*, and I want nothing more than to slit the man's throat and give him a lesson in proper spelling. Just as Merissa said there would be, there's a book-sized window with closed shutters. A wooden plaque hangs from a nail, reading THE MASTER IS OUT, and I shake my head and flip it around.

The other side also says THE MASTER IS OUT.

There's a bell cord, but it's easy enough to follow its path up to the eaves and see the bucket of something or other poised to fall on the head of anyone foolish enough to attempt to ring it.

"Bugger it all," I mutter.

Reaching into my pocket, I pull out not a bit of magic powder or a dastardly device...but a simple letter opener that doubles as a dagger in a pinch. Without a word of warning, I jigger the shutters open, careful to hold my face away should anyone be waiting within to give me a well-deserved punch in the nose.

The wagon's interior is dark and still, thick and heavy with the sort of constantly smothered fire favored by arthritic aunts, and ripe with a dozen smells, none appetizing. I see no sign of this Master Bailey.

"What the blast, cretin?"

I'm so startled that I stumble back and only barely manage to turn it into a courtly bow. The voice comes from everywhere at once, and I finally pinpoint it to a phonograph's brass flower under the wagon's roof. Ah, yes. The speaker Merissa mentioned. How quaint.

"My lord, I've brought you the grandest magic show in the land of Sang," I start, but a juicy laugh ends in a clearing throat, an oddly tinny quaver through the speaker. I barely manage to dodge sideways as the glob of tobacco lobs out of the window and splatters in the dust.

"Got a magician," he says. "Don't need two. You're welcome to duel the other fellow, if you need a job bad enough. But I suspect..." He trails off, and I can feel the cat's claws extend. "If you really are the grandest magician in Sang, I'm sure you're off for greener pastures than this little caravan, eh?"

"I'm not much of a one for pastures, sir. But you'll find me a Jack-of-all-trades. Ringmaster, acrobat, sideshow barker..."

"Keep going, lad. You'll eventually get to the bit where you're poking at trash with a pointy stick." Deep in his dragon's lair, I can imagine him chewing his tobacco and thinking on it. And it's not safe to let haughty hermits think too much when a fellow's livelihood is at stake.

"Bring me your magician, then," I say, chin up. "I could do with a good duel."

The bastard cackles like a hen and spits again. "You'll battle him on the stage tonight. Winner gets his wagon. Loser bunks with the wolf boy and shovels manure behind Merissa's beasts. If he lives."

I don't even have to think. "Done. And the name is—"

"Don't bother," he says. "I don't care about names until I'm having them painted on the sides of wagons."

My NEXT STOP is the dining car. It's easy enough to find—they always are. Just look for braces of dead bludbunnies hanging from hooks on the side of the wagon, waiting to become tomorrow's stew. I'm doubly disappointed when I step inside: Merissa isn't here, and it's clear where my people stand in the hierarchy. Just like in a city, the Bludmen are firmly corralled into a black-painted corner while the humans and daimons have windows, clean booths, and a buffet of whatever offal they desire. I see only two Bludmen, or rather, one Bludman with two heads, all four eyes fastened on me and glittering madly. I nod and head for the cauldron of blood and a tower of chipped teacups to make it seem like a civilized sort of drink instead of liquid flesh sold by the stoppered tube.

"What're you lookin' at, mate?" A half-daimon the color of a November sky twirls a long railroad nail between his fingers, pointing it at me when I look him up and down by the beverage dispenser.

"Lunch," I say. "Or are you a daimon that feeds on idiocy?"

He pokes the nail into his nose as if storing it for later and readies himself for fisticuffs, but his venomous tail has been cut off. Amputation is the price daimons pay to work for humans in cabarets and caravans, and without his tail's magic and stinger, he can't do anything more than leap around like a lizard. At least all I sacrifice is, temporarily, my freedom.

Beside him, a dark red daimon lady in a dancing costume catches his sleeve. "Don't be a fool," she says. "Can't you feel the desire flowing off him? He'll tear you to pieces, and gladly."

I give her a nod of respect. "I am hungry for my place in the world, madam. But I'm aiming a good bit higher than the freak tent." I see it register in her eyes—she knows me or has at least heard my name. There's nothing for it, so I stick out my hand. "Criminy Stain, at your service."

With a wry grin, she lets me kiss the back of her wrist. "Mademoiselle Caprice, dancing mistress. Charmed, monsieur. I've heard tell of your show. But we've a magician here already, you know."

"I was informed as such and will be murdering him tonight."

She takes back her hand and tucks a fist under her chin, thinking. "Tricky. He's rather good, you see."

"But he's not currently in this room?"

"He is not."

I select one blood vial, and when no one stops me, a second. The top teacup is chipped, so I rub a finger over it, muttering under my breath until the porcelain is unblemished. "If you've any ideas regarding how to best this magician, you'll find me around," I say.

She gives a polite nod. "Ah, but monsieur, is it better to help the devil you know or the devil you don't?"

I let my eyes twinkle at her and doff my hat. "It's better to make friends with the more devilish of the two devils."

And since we both know that silly, arbitrary lines are drawn in this wagon, I've no choice but to head for the blackened corner where I belong. When I run my own caravan, there will be no such division. Fear does stupid things to a soft man, and Old Bailey is softer and more fearful than most. Judging by the crafty, sullen looks on the two-headed Bludman I'm about to dominate, there's an undercurrent of dangerous neglect over the truly murderous, and it's almost ironic that anyone would expect a simple coat of black paint to keep real monsters in their place.

"Is this seat taken?" I tilt my head to the bench opposite him. Them? Damn, but proper grammar wasn't made to address multiple heads.

"Depends. You as frilly as you look?" snarls one head, and the other just raises a brow.

I gently place the teacup and blood vials on the scarred black table. "If you'd care to go outside and have your throats ripped out, I'd be glad to accommodate you, but I'm afraid I've only the one handkerchief and I'm going to drink my lunch first."

"I'm Catarrh. That's Quincy. Who the hell are you?"

A vial in each fist, I pop the corks with my thumbs and let the warm blood mix in my cup.

"Only allowed one vial per meal, new meat," Catarrh says, and Quincy chitters.

"I'm Criminy Stain, and I don't take orders well. How do you get away with it?"

As I sip my blood, and it's not bad blood at all, Quincy chews his sharpened nails and Catarrh considers me more carefully, and I know now which head I'll always have to watch out for.

"Get away with what?" Catarrh says, feigning innocence and failing utterly.

I toss down the rest of my blood and snatch his poorly tied cravat in my fist, jerking him across the table. My other fist smashes my teacup into Quincy's face as my fangs find Catarrh's neck and settle there, for just a moment, for just long enough, in the darkest sort of promise. I slowly draw a red line across his throat with a tooth and toss him back against the bench.

"You drink from customers. And yet you still have a job. And that tells me that whoever runs this caravan is a damned fool who's scared of you. I think you'll find that I am neither."

It's a tense moment, and I tap my talons on the table, one-two-three. Quincy sniffles to himself, trying to lick the cuts on his cheeks, and Catarrh touches the scratch on his neck and breathes hard through his nose for a moment before whispering, "I submit."

"Good." I snatch Catarrh's teacup and drain the dregs, exposing my throat in the sort of way that tells another predator that it is not now or ever a threat to me.

Catarrh and Quincy watch, sullen and slumped against the back of the bench.

"I didn't submit," Quincy snarls, and I set down his brother's teacup and lean forwards with a ferociously mad smile and the all-too-sharp letter opener I've just whipped from my vest. "But I do. I do!" he whimpers.

I relax and nod. "Smart lads. Now, tell me about this other magician."

They shrug, which tells me all that I need to know.

"The Great Phaedro," Catarrh says, flapping a hand. "Whoopty-doodley."

"Not great," Quincy mutters, still compulsively rubbing the place where I took a divot out of his pimpled cheek with his own cup.

"What's his specialty?"

Quincy snickers, and Catarrh says, "Cutting girls in half. What's yours?"

"Cutting magicians in half."

But the small hairs on my neck rise up. I don't just cut girls in half; I make them disappear completely.

IF THIS CARAVAN is like the other two in which I've worked, then no matter how poorly it's run, things will start to warm up just as the sun is setting. Sure enough, some of the more talented carnivalleros who actually have jobs are practicing, as they should be. There's a sprightly old man on the tightrope, gray and wrinkled but still wiry as the twisted metal under his slippers. Far below him, on the ground, sit two small girls in outlandishly bright costumes, doing their sums on a chalkboard as they share stale popcorn. A middle-aged lady with horse teeth checks her flea circus with a monocle screwed over her eye, while a young blonde Bludwoman slips into a tailpiece and prepares to launch herself into an unkempt mermaid's aquarium. A patchy, defanged wolf boy is manacled to a stake in the ground, which he's trying to dig out with bloody paws.

Further on, I meet a troupe of daimon acrobats and, surprisingly, a strong woman with arms that each weigh more than my entire body. Mademoiselle Caprice dances with a handsome Bludman covered in tattoos, while a voluptuous dwarf lady does her makeup in a cracked mirror. The Freak Tent is at the end, a cluster of fraying pavilions that sets me frowning when I find the entrance unguarded.

It's bad enough that this Bailey fellow never leaves his wagon, but if he doesn't have a second-in-command capable of maintaining order, he's just begging me to snatch this languishing jewel from his crusty grasp. I duck under the striped canvas and nearly run into the light blue daimon I met in the dining wagon as he double-checks his bed of nails.

"Want to have a curl-up?" he says mockingly, and I try not to roll my eyes.

"I know the trick, fool. If you want to impress me, learn to hammer a nail into your eye."

"That's impossible," he says, and I laugh.

"Give me a nail and a hammer then, if you'd care to wager."

With a rude snort, he picks up his hammer and tosses it in the air, catching it expertly. "What are the terms, then?"

"If I can successfully hammer a nail into my eye, you'll stop being a prat and accept that I'm most likely going to stick around and one day become your boss."

"And if you end up in an eye patch?" He hands me a nail, and I grin, because there are a dozen ways he could've sabotaged me, and he's far too stupid to have even tried.

"If I lose, I'll give you a spell to make your skin brighter."

Considering a water-colored half-daimon's skin is his greatest shame, I take a certain joy in watching his eyes take on a holy shine. The brighter the daimon, the better the show, they say, and it's no wonder this poor faded fellow is so cranky.

"You're on, mate," he says.

We shake hands, and I hold the small nail to the corner of my left eye. Three sharp and dramatic knocks, and it's lodged flawlessly. I hold out my arms and shout, "Tada!"

"That's impossible," he says, half in awe and half starving to possess my trick.

"That's five years in the freak tent," I say. But I make a little show of prying the nail out because no geek deserves to feel out-geeked in his own domain. Poor lad just needs better training, a firmer hand, and some manners, all of which I'd be glad to give him once I've murdered a few people. Tossing the nail to him, I balance the hammer on my nose and say, "Now, what can you tell me about this Phaedro fellow?"

The daimon's yellow goat eyes go all shifty as he turns the nail over in watery blue hands, still hunting for an illusion that isn't there. "Doesn't seem right to tell a gent's weaknesses to a stranger."

"My name is Criminy Stain," I say, holding out a hand. "And I might be strange, but that's just part of my charm."

"Laraby." We shake hands and I return his hammer, and he finally makes his decision to not infuriate someone who clearly knows how to handle weapons.

"Phaedro's act is mostly illusion. When he cuts a lass in half, it's the legless lady from the third booth down in the Freak Tent. When he makes someone disappear, it's a daimon with good control over color-changing. And when a bludbunny pops out of his hat, it's because he keeps a toothless bludbunny in his hat all the time."

"So, he has no real magic?"

Laraby shrugs. "Not much, by my count. But he mostly keeps to himself to himself. Seen him among the other Bludmen, from time to time, but never really talked to 'im. Now, about that trick with the nail?"

"Business first. But I do appreciate your help, and so I'll thank you with this." I pull a tiny bag out of my pocket, for my jacket has hundreds of such pockets sewn into the lining, and I've memorized exactly where everything is and have the proper bits and bobs apportioned for just such an occasion. "Place one grain—only one, mind you—on your tongue, and you'll find it far easier to hold onto brighter colors, at least for a few hours at a time."

He takes the small bag, pokes it with a finger the color of melting snow. "Not permanent, then?"

"Sorry, lad," I say, walking on. "Nothing is."

FURTHER EXPLORATION OF the Freak Tent shows me nothing new. I've seen all these freaks before and in better form. The dwarf is drunk and abusive, the wolf boy has sores from his manacles, the legless lady wants more than the going rate for being sawn in half, and the two-headed boy simply sits sullenly on a small chaise and stares. Pizzazz is lacking and morale is nonexistent.

I smile. This place wants me, needs me.

Outside again, I turn right to see what the other side of the wagon train holds and find...nothing. Blank spaces and darkness. I guess I know now how Catarrh and Quincy get their dessert—by dragging customers back here and charming them before releasing them, dizzy and confused and down a few pints of blood, back into the well-lit crowds. The wildlife creeps close on the dark side of the train, thanks to the lack of lights. The grasses crunch and whisper as bluddeer and bludbunnies stalk and hop and drool and wait, mere inches from innocent flesh. There's not even a sign warning the audience not to come this way. This traditional setup is foolish, but so are most things that need changing. It feels good, pissing on the nearest wagon. That's how we predators claim things, after all.

Back in the light, I find Merissa working a white horse and fuss with my cravat. I haven't seen a mirror since I left my old home, much less an ewer or a wardrobe wagon. Not that she's watching me—she has eyes only for the white mare, which has been brushed to an incandescent sheen, her long mane and tail as white as driven snow as she trots majestically in the circle, her big red eyes pinned lovingly to the delicate lady holding the golden rope and a long, flexible whip.

Merissa's eyes shoot to me, and her brow wrinkles adorably before she looks behind her. Standing there is a comically gothic fellow, slighter than me and wrapped in a long, black cloak more than a little like mine, although the cut of his is out of date and the quality is shabbier. I had my cloak lined in emerald green to match my waistcoat, but this fellow's cape is in a traditional blood red, as if the world couldn't otherwise tell that he was a Bludman. In all respects, he is less than me. A little shorter, a little narrower about the shoulders, his slicked-back hair a bland brown, his eyes a muddier blue enhanced by a cool rage that I can feel, even with a girl and a horse between us.

Oh, but this is going to be fun.

"What an enchanting creature," I say, stepping to Merissa's side and moving fluidly with her as she trains the horse.

"Don't flatter me while I'm working," she mutters, but the corner of her mouth twitches just so.

"I assure you I was speaking of the horse. But where is the one from this morning? Kali?"

Her eyes flick to me, a ripple in an emerald-green pond, and her smile is suddenly genuine. "How did you know it wasn't her?"

I cross my arms to better broadcast my muscular superiority over the weedy gent standing out of the horse's orbit. "This one has longer fetlocks and her mane falls mainly to the left. This morning's Kali was younger, probably still has a hand to grow, and her mane fell to the right."

"Well played, Stain. You're correct. This is Kali's new partner, Fausta."

"I am curious as to how two bludmares can be coerced into cooperation. It was my understanding that they would battle to the death, should they meet in the wild."

Her laugh sends ripples of want up my arms, her voice as warm as puddled blood. "They would if they did, sure enough. But I've developed a new technique for fostering sisterhood." She puts the rope and whip in my hands. "Keep her trotting, please." With a dramatic rip, her skirts fly off and flutter to the ground at Phaedro's feet. Her legs are revealed, clad in green suede breeches and high, padded boots. She watches the horse for a moment, and I tap the mare's hip gently with the whip before she can falter. With a nod, Merissa skips, catches Fausta's mane, and swings up onto her back. The horse doesn't break her speed, shows no indication that she's been mastered other than an elegant bowing of her head as if to a greater queen.

"I force a blood exchange," Merissa says, deftly leaping to her feet to stand on the horse's back. Her voice doesn't even break; she might as well be standing on a chaise. "Just a few drops, and they become sisters, intimately connected in body and mind. You see, I've picketed Kali where she can watch Fausta go through her paces, and she's absorbing it like a prodigy with an abacus."

I glance quickly to the direction in which she's pointing and see the magnificent young beast tethered to the ground and watching us all, her fine head cocked to the side inquisitively.

If you gave the mare a quill and a pair of pince-nez, she might be mistaken for a studious clerk taking notes. Damned if Merissa isn't right, is all I'm saying.

"I didn't know horses possessed such keen intelligence." I use the whip to nudge Fausta back out to the end of the rope before Merissa has to ask.

"Anyone can see that hubris is your sin of choice, Stain." She grasps the horse's mane in one hand and lifts one leg high overhead in a ballerina's flawless arabesque that knocks the breath right out of me.

"Oh, but I don't believe in sin at all, Merissa."

The horse snorts on her behalf, and Merissa's leg gracefully falls. She doesn't speak again until she's turned to face me, boot toes curled over the horse's spine, hands on her hips, Kali's gallop of no more consequence than the waves lapping at a great ship of conquest.

"Oh, but I do," she says, nearly a purr.

And for the first time, I consider changing my beliefs.

Our eyes lock, and I realize I'm dizzy and on fire and possibly falling for this tiny virago who can clearly master the most ferocious of beasts. She breaks off the look of longing with a sharp nod and catapults off the horse's back in a flip that leaves her standingon the ground as the horse slows to a walk and stares at me expectantly.

"Put her picket by Kali's, would you?"

She doesn't wait for an answer, just picks up her fallen skirts and sashays towards a wagon painted the dark, secret green of her eyes with *Mistress Merissa and her Mesmerizing Mares* scrolling across the side. The Great Phaedro is gone completely, and I wonder at which point our viciously mischievous conversational foreplay drove him away to snivel somewhere else.

As I've nothing better to do, I picket the great beast and pat her withers, for which she gives me an appropriately withering stare.

"Is being ridden by her as lovely as I dream it would be, mate?"

The horse snorts and turns her rump to me.

"Who'd have guessed you were such a genteel soul?" I say.

And I laugh, for the same has been said of me.

5

I spend the next few hours wishing for my library of grimoires and two more pocket-honeycombed coats filled with powders and talismans. The only book I brought with me was a family heirloom, and no matter how I hunt and peck, I can't find anything in it for killing rival magicians. Although I in no way doubt my ability to best this Phaedro, I always prefer to stack several decks in my favor. If nothing else, I've got my cloak, which has already proven useful for disposing of inconveniences, even if Phaedro might be a bit too tall to banish completely. I suppose his lower legs wouldn't cause too much of a ruckus if left behind in a conjuring gone wrong. After all, tall boots look pretty much the same with or without feet still in them.

Without a wagon of my own, I head for a wooded copse on the other side of the caravan from the one where I met Merissa. I need to concentrate, not sigh longingly at her artistic splatters of ruby-red blood. I already know that birch trees will forever remind me of seeing her there, small and bright as a jewel in the snow.

Even though it wasn't snowing at the time. In my mind's eye, it was, you see.

These woods, sadly, have been ruined. A square tunnel violates the sanctity of the trees in the exact shape of the bus tanks that carry customers from the city over the hill—Shrewsbury, I think it is. And typical of Pinkies, instead of going around this quiet, lovely wood, they've barreled straight through the middle of it, leaving crushed branches and a few smashed bludsquirrels in their wake. I suppose I should be glad I don't have thorns catching in my cloak and branches aiming for my eyes, but I can't help hating how they treat the world so carelessly, as if they owned it. So like a prey species that's never had to manage a population responsibly.

I aim for a tumbledown wall of gray stones and place my coat, grimoire, and cloak on the weathered rocks to take inventory of the weapons in my arsenal. Anxious as I am for tonight's show, I've never fought to the death before using anything but my teeth and claws, when the beast inside me takes over and sings for blood. If I'm too sudden, too cruel, the audience won't have time to clap and Merissa will think me a great brute. But a wise man never gives his enemy time to find his footing and pull something surprising and clever out of his bum, so I'll have to time it just right for maximum pomp and annihilation.

I say my prayers to Aztarte, bite my finger, and let a drop of my blood fall onto the raw black soil. I want what I have always wanted: my own caravan and someone to rule it by my side. Merissa is everything I've ever wanted in a mate: beauty, humor, confidence, murderousness. If I can best Phaedro and dispose of Bailey, I can have both of my dreams in one fell swoop. I'm sure my goddess understands.

As the setting sun paints the countryside in broad brushstrokes of orange and purple, I draw on my coat and cape, every weapon I possess placed perfectly for success. The tanks are rumbling towards my quiet wood, so I hurry back to the caravan to mingle with the carnivalleros before the audience is disgorged and the show begins. Say it's nerves and I'll slit your throat in a smile; I just prefer to be among my own people, is all.

The lazy buggers have finally left their shoddy wagons to prepare for the impending show, and I can't hide my moue of distaste at how all of this should've been done already, not to mention that they've wasted one full side of the caravan train and could stand to dream bigger.

On my way to Merissa's wagon, where I'm hoping to catch her for a tender but charged moment before the show proper, something stops me. It's a wee, high voice calling from a strange tent I didn't see earlier. I have to step over the hooks between two wagon cars to reach it. Whereas all of Bailey's other tents are gaily striped and topped with little flags, this one is a violent sort of orange and conical. The fabric glimmers and almost seems to melt under the sunset's scrutiny, and a peculiar, all-too-human odor wafts out.

"Good sir, my cheese has something to tell you."

That catches my attention. It's not very often that anything in this world surprises me in a not unpleasant way, but...

The winsome creature behind the table can't be older than nine, human and pale as a blossom with dark hair in tight pigtails. She's done up in the most regrettable costume, an older woman's skirts and jacket hanging off her and dragging the ground. A circlet of flowers sits on her head, and her face is deadly serious, far more serious than any child of any species has any right to be. And I can't tell if she's human or Bludman because I can't smell her.

I poke my head in the door and sniff. "I'm sorry, but did you say...cheese?"

"Yes, sir." She spreads small hands in fingerless gloves. "My cheese knows all."

The table is indeed spread with a wide variety of the edible substance I know only through my ridiculous fondness for books. To be quite honest, I had no idea how many forms and facets could be found in a cheese, but there are round ones, tall ones, pointy ones, gooey ones, and mountainous mounds riddled with holes big enough to hide a bludrat in. The smell is wholesome and greasy and not altogether unpleasant, but as none of these cheeses have mouths to speak, I'm not sure what the sweet creature intends.

Each cheese, I note, is stuck through with a knife sized just to fit in the girl's fingers.

"And how do I access this knowledge, dear child?" I say politely.

She holds out a small hand, regal as a queen. "Cross my palm with copper."

I duck into her tent, and it's like walking into a glowing ember. There's a small brazier on the table, lanterns and beeswax candles all around, reflecting off the gold and orange and aged ivory hues of the cheeses, and I can't help thinking that even in a life as long and strange as my own, this is a particularly unique and unexpected experience. I reach out to touch a pierced lantern showing the old fable of Little Red Riding Hood, with a wolf stalking a hooded child among a scattering of stars. It spins under my fingertips, making light dance on the tent walls. When I look at the girl, she grins without fangs.

In the silence, I listen for the cheese to make a noise, to speak. It does not.

"The copper, sir," she reminds me, and I chuckle and give her a silver instead.

Her widened eyes betray her, but she tries like hell to cover her surprise and pleasure. The silver disappears, and she produces a long-handled spoon, fire-blackened and bent.

With great authority, she says, "Select your cheese."

"They're all the same to me, love." My fang-disclosing grin aims for a shared joke and not a threat.

Her head falls forwards, and she intones with all seriousness, "The cheese will call you."

And damned if I don't believe her. With a shrug, I hold out my hand and slowly move my palm over the table of foodstuff. A range of strange odors assaults me, and I detect everything from nuts and fruit and ale and chocolate and mold to a scent reminiscent of the inside of a goat's mouth. But then, the strangest thing happens. I smell something...amazing. A mix of fine red wine, crushed vines, wildness, and sex. It's entirely separate from the cheeses, has utterly nothing to do with cheese, and I'm so surprised that I turn to look over my shoulder to see if someone else has followed me into the tent wearing altogether too much decadent perfume.

There is no one there. Just me dand the waif and her cheeses. My hand hovers over a boring little wedge of creamy ivory. When I move my hand, the delicious smell disappears, but so long as my hand is over this one, plain cheese...ah, the scent! I bend closer, noting a small tag that reads Leigh Cheese, but the block itself smells nothing like the scent that screams to me of dreams and promises and victory.

"What the bloody hell was that?" I say.

The girl finally smiles, a deep dimple in her cheek. "That was the cheese whispering, sir. Let's see what it wishes to say." She holds out the spoon. "Please slice off enough to fit in the ladle."

"Fair enough, lass." I take the spoon, pluck the knife from the cheese, and whittle off an obliging corner, marveling at the peculiar texture. There's a fleshiness to it, but a crumbliness, too. After stabbing the knife back into its slot, I hold out the spoon to her, handle first.

She takes it with a queenly nod and holds it over the brazier. I step closer despite myself, fascinated by this interplay. I've had my fortune told in tea leaves, in love lines, in the curled skins of apples I've never tasted. I've thrown bones and scried in the messy guts of half-dead bludrabbits. But I've never found the answers I seek, and the fortunetellers all seem to share the same sly smile at some knowledge they hold back for reasons of their own, and not for lack of my coin. One old crone just laughed and said, "You're asking the wrong fortuneteller, me boyo," and I never asked another.

As I watch, mesmerized, the wedge of cheese melts into a bubbling puddle.

"Look into the cheese, sir. Let your heart ask the question your mouth fears to speak."

My mouth doesn't fear anything, but I respect her pageantry too much to break the spell. The question at the top of my mind, of course, is "Will I best Phaedro and take this caravan for myself?" but the words I hear chime up from my soul are far different, and as her eyes roll back into her head and she tips the molten cheese onto a black marble slab, I think, "What will it take to truly satisfy my hunger for conquest and love?"

The slab must be charmed to coldness, for the cheese coagulates almost instantly, reminding me more than a little of blood clotting on winter-frosted cobbles. I think I see shapes in it, but I look to the girl, hoping the cheese doesn't reveal me to be a romantic.

Her eyes pop open, and she looks down and smiles. "What does it take? What it always takes. Magic, time, tenacity, sacrifice. One will happen soon, but the other won't happen for decades. Your love comes with rubies in a birch forest, naked and unafraid." For just a second, her somber expression breaks, and she points at a long, pointy streak of cheese. "This arrow is going to hurt," she says quietly, as if she's not supposed to mention that bit. "And there's a witch."

"Good to know," I murmur, trying to see anything in the streaks of gloppy white goo. There are no hints, no symbols, no runes. Merely fetid bits of teatmilk from overwrought cows, and so how can it speak in anything but opaque riddles?

With quick, practiced gestures, she scrapes the cheese off the slab and into a bucket on the floor. When she stands again, her face is a professional mask belied only by the quick replacement of a fallen strap on her gown.

"Thank you," she says with great solemnity, and I know well enough when I'm being dismissed. After all, the real customers will be here soon.

I give her my most gracious bow and pull another copper from behind my ear to place on her marble slab. "Oh, no, my little one. Thank you." I'm about to leave, but something stops me. "What does the cheese tell *you*, love?" I ask.

Her eyes twinkle with a cunning streak. "That when you get what you want, I'll get what I want."

"And what's that?"

She smiles sweetly. "What everyone wants: revenge and freedom."

"Aren't you a bit young to need revenge?"

With a giggle, she flicks aside the back curtain of her tent. "We're none of us as young as we seem," she says, and then she's gone.

Outside in the darkening night, I realize that I received no answers about my showdown with Phaedro the Great. But all the other bits can't come true unless I live through this bit, can they? I know too much to ever believe I'll lose this battle. If love comes in a birch forest with ruby splatters of blood, then love is a doll-like Bludwoman riding a saddleless horse, unafraid of anything. The circus, I suppose, will simply take more time. But the girl's cheese confirmed my suspicions: I'll have it all, one day. I just have to kill Phaedro first.

Merissa was right. Pride is definitely my favorite sin, but wrath and lust call me, too.

6

They're waiting for me, and I can only hope I don't stink of cheese. No man who is master of his fate should ever reek of cheese. A dab of powder from pocket number eighty-two renders me odorless, and I'm dabbing cologne from pocket eighty-three against my pulse as I near the crowd.

"Wizard duel at eight o'clock sharp," Bailey screeches over the speaker. "See some rude and foppish young upstart battle Phaedro the Great! An extra copper buys a stageside seat."

Sure enough, the mad fools have set up a corral of velvet ropes around a stage. The wagon behind it is indigo blue, the stage uneven and lined inexpertly with steel-cupped lanterns. No one has noticed my approach, as they're all focused on a gold-and-blue sarcophagus standing upright in the middle of the stage, its arms crossed and its eyes unblinking.

I draw in a deep breath and shake my head as I take on my mantle of power. At just the right moment, I throw out my arms and appear in a puff of smoke, my face set in wicked determination.

As if on cue, the crowd turns to me and gasps, parting before me like the Red Sea, the sarcophagus utterly forgotten. I stalk through and among them, cape billowing, head down at the angle between glorious and furious. Near the front of the stage, Merissa stands, arms crossed, inscrutable as ever in a deep red gown that displays the perfect curve of her neck and shoulders. If I look at her too long, I'll lose focus, so I merely raise a dark, dashing eyebrow at her and leap to the stage in a swirl of black and emerald, cutting through a puff of lavender smoke.

The crowd applauds and whistles, and for just a moment, I know a daimon's hunger for attention and adulation as I drink in their wonder.

A spotlight cuts to the blue and gold sarcophagus as tinny music rumbles over the speaker, and the crowd turns to gape at the papier mâché coffin that surely holds my rival. Before he can do whatever he has planned, I plant a boot firmly in the thing's chest and kick it to the ground, where it crumples and reveals a neat hole cut in the boards. Phaedro's head pokes up like an idiot mole, and I have to stop myself from kicking his face off his spindly neck like a bloody football. I toss a packet onto the sarcophagus and it catches fire, glowing green and throwing sparks. In moments, the gaudy prop is completely gone.

"Your turn," I say, throwing out a dramatic arm, and Phaedro disappears in his own puff of smoke as the curtains swoop closed.

"Show-off." Merissa has somehow hopped onto the stage in her voluminous skirts. "That wasn't fair."

"Of course it wasn't fair, love. It's a duel. Please tell me you're not his assistant." I check through my pockets, palm a few possibilities. "I've more respect for your horses than a ninny like the Great Phaedro."

"You've been here less than a day, Stain. You've never spoken to him. It's the height of savage ignorance, really, the way you sauntered in and decided to take over a system that worked very well. I might venture to say you're acting rather... human."

I put a hand over my chest. "Such insults from my lady love."

She stares delicious daggers at me. "I never claimed to be a lady, and I certainly never agreed to be your love. No promises were made. Had I known how much trouble you would cause, I'd have killed you and left you for the horses." With each whispered word, she steps closer until she's right up in my face, a finger jabbing into my chest. I've never been so enamored, nor so conflicted.

She tosses her chin and steps back, cool again. "Go on and best him, if you can. You'll never own me, just as I'll never own those horses." And then she's gone, taking my heart with her.

With a jangle of rings, the curtain goes up, and I realize that I look like a moonstruck boy, staring after the lady who's rejected his clumsy attentions. And so I do what any boy does then: I show off.

With a bow to the crowd, I sweep off my tall topper and withdraw three flaming torches and a snow-white bludbunny with blood-red eyes. As I juggle them, a merry tune plays from a small, enchanted box in one of my many pockets. The rabbit snarls as it tumbles; this one in particular hates the party hat I've charmed onto its silky head. The flames change color, from the usual orange to ice blue to hot purple and spring green. The crowd claps and whistles, and I grin. I have enough of these petty tricks to keep them happy for hours, and at this rate, Phaedro's incompetence and lack of showmanship might force me to do just that. Poor weasel's probably pissing himself under the stage.

When I sense the audience's attention begin to wane, I let all the flames and bunnies fall back into my hat, *boom boom boom boom*, and sweep it back onto my head in a dashing bow. They go mad, simply mad, and I drink it in. And that's when he throws his first fireball.

I didn't even notice Phaedro standing there, wrapped in his cape like a bat, but I feel a hot burst of pain explode against my vest, catching my fine cloak on fire, and I stumble back, snarling.

A second ball of fire smacks me in the stomach, because let's be honest, snarling doesn't really stop that sort of thing from happening. I swat it to the ground, stomp out the fire licking my cloak, and tackle Phaedro before he can throw a third one.

The scuffle is feral and rough, all magic and showmanship forgotten as claws tear for tender eyes and veins. Our teeth snap as we tumble and growl, each bite landing on air as we writhe. I'm slightly bigger than him, slightly stronger than him, a hell of a lot tougher than him, and yet I'm not gaining the ground I should be. Strikes that should rend him in half only make him fight harder. A claw to the jugular doesn't yield the spurting geyser of blud that I crave. His wounds seem to close, his eyes always a hairsbreadth away from my talons.

The crowd, at least, is eating it up, roaring their approval and pounding their fists on the stage as they place bets. I find myself defending more than aggressing, a situation forever untenable. And so I double my onslaught and force him onto his back, my claws poised to scoop his guts from his belly like blood sorbet from a porcelain dish.

Something cracks in the air, and suddenly, I'm unable to breathe.

My neck—something around it—my fingers claw for it, to loosen it.

A whip.

Merissa's whip.

The world is going dark, and the curtain is skittering closed, and I yank the taut leather and feel the floor thud under my knees as Merissa falls. Underneath me, Phaedro whispers incantations in a language I don't know, his eyes closed. Just before my vision gives out, I make good on my promise and swipe out his throat with my claws.

The last thing I feel is the rasp of his raw spine against my fingertips and the chest under me exhale and still.

7

esterday, I would've told you that only weak little prats pass out during times of duress, but that was before I'd been throttled by a horsewoman's whip. Today, I would confess that the aftereffects of a nearly crushed trachea feels a lot like a cravat tied far too tightly by someone who hates you. I can also tell you that Phaedro's wagon is nice, if shabby, and that his bed is too soft for satisfying lovemaking. Still, it's better than waking up out in the woods by a trash heap or staked on a pyre, surrounded by an angry crowd.

"Awake finally?" Merissa asks, hovering over me like a delicately fanged angel.

"I had the strangest dream," I say. "See, I was a stallion, and a beautiful lady lassoed me…"

"You were going to kill him," she says, eyes downcast as she sits on the edge of the bed in a black chemise, not quite close enough to touch, her auburn hair all glossy perfection. "In front of the crowd. It's bad for business. I had to stall your bloodshed until the curtain was closed."

I taste her lie on my open mouth and smile.

"All's well that ends well, eh, love? Although if I'm to live here, I'll need a bigger bed, more bookshelves, and a desk with a few more bitty drawers. That Phaedro fellow's decorating style was a bit grim."

I vastly prefer caravan wagons divided into two portions, a bedroom and a parlor, but this one is a large, lightless rectangle with all the appeal of a crypt. The out-of-date wallpaper is purple with damask gates, while the heavy, black tables and chairs and trunks crowd together like a meeting of humpbacked witches. The lamps are turned down, the coverlet so black, I can't see my legs.

And I, a grown Bludman, am half dressed under a dead man's blanket like an invalid, which is utterly unacceptable, even if my throat feels like a cracked egg and there are two burned spots on my torso that will most likely carry scars for the rest of my life. I bolt upright gracefully, throwing over the covers and standing before my darkling nurse can protest. The ground wobbles under my feet.

Or does it?

It does. Because the wagon is on the move.

"Where are we for?" I ask.

Merissa smiles. "Southpool, Deadpool, Blackpool."

"And where is Phaedro the Not As Great as Advertised?"

She blows air like an angry horse. "Cremated in a small jar. Was that really necessary?"

I reach for her hand, and although it's rigid at her side, she softens to let me lift it. I press her palm to make her fingers splay and trace the tender line up her thumb's Mound of Venus, straight up the white talon, to the tip.

"We're predators, my sweet. And cheetahs don't change their spots. Especially when they're rather fond of being cheetahs. If I hadn't killed him, he'd have killed me."

A small chuckle as she snatches her hand back. "That sounds like the Phaedro I know."

"The Phaedro you *knew*." I step closer, close enough to smell the scent of violets and musk drifting about her like clouds in a graveyard, overlaid with the warm, meaty scent of horse. "And now you can know me. You were his sometimes assistant. Will you be mine?"

I pull her to her feet. She sways back and forth, seductive as hell, and looks up at me through dark lashes. White skin, black eyes, ruby lips; she's the birch forest, and I'm the beast caught in her branches. "Depends on what's involved, I suppose."

"First things first, love." I cup her jaw and bend to kiss her, slow and sweet and deep and dark. If she didn't know me before this moment, she knows me now. Her breath catches, and she sighs and softens, kissing me back.

After thorough exploration, I pull back and nip her lip. "Secondly, perhaps you could help me rip down these burial shrouds and find something a little less atrocious for the walls. I'm going to need some real light. And we'll want the painter to start on the wagon."

"Oh, well, complete redecoration on a moving train. That's not much to ask." She runs a hand down the wall with an unreadable expression on her face. "That's how it works, then? You show up, murder someone, and change every detail to suit yourself?"

My smile is wolfish, purposefully so.

"Exactly, love. Exactly."

"And will you ask the same of me?"

I grasp her waist and pull her close, but only because she lets me.

"I don't change things that are already perfect," I say.

And she kisses me, a small peck on the cheek.

"Neither do I, Stain. Neither do I."

I'M FULLY DRESSED and back at Bailey's window, but this time, it bangs open before I can assault it with my knife. The train has stopped in the middle of nowhere, which means everyone else is taking a break in the dining car, enjoying some fresh air before we resume travel and they're all locked in their wagons again. But I've already tossed down four vials of blood—for Phaedro's are mine now, are they not? And I'm ready for my next fight.

"What now?" the voice barks through the speaker. "You got what you wanted. Quite a show."

I incline my head a scant bit. He might be in charge, but he's still a human, after all.

"I wish to make some changes in my lodging."

As anticipated, my words are welcomed with a glob of tobacco that I easily dodge.

"And who made you the bloody magistrate? Wagon ain't good enough for you? Well, we'd best be trundling off for London so the kitty-puss can stretch out on a silk cushion."

I sigh. "If you're done, I was just hoping for a few more lanterns and a bigger mirror. That Phaedro fellow had all the panache of a blind bat."

His growl is tinny through the speaker. "Have someone show you the prop wagon. If you can't find what you want in there, you can find it your own damn self. You might be a murderer, Mr. Stain, but you don't scare me."

"If requesting a lamp is akin to murder, I respectfully hope you'll consider reexamining your ethics," I say drily, and the shutters slam closed.

After checking the time, I hurry to the prop wagon. I can probably dig out some supplies before the train starts up again, and it's customary to blow a horn or otherwise alert the carnivalleros before the train starts to move, if one doesn't want to accidentally leave one's employees behind to be eaten by rabbits. Considering the smaller size of Bailey's show, the prop wagon takes up half of the costume wagon, both of which are ruled over by a vicious old Bludwoman who resembles a vulture. I've avoided her up until now, and if she's in the dining room during my little raid, I shan't be sorry. When my polite knock goes unanswered, I impolitely jigger the door with my lockpicks and hurry inside.

I light a lantern by the door and hold it up to a kingdom of junk. It's jumbled, of course. That's the whole point of a prop wagon. Most of the furniture and equipment is damaged somehow: chairs missing a leg, a broken guitar, a dented tuba, a tragically cross-eyed mechanical bear smeared with oil. I push further in, knowing very well that the best things are often the hardest ones to find.

Props tower overhead, and I can't take the lantern any farther without risking fire. At my whispered word, a small light blooms from my fingertips. I abandon the lantern and press on. A chaise and a large box are shoved together like a barricade, which means someone is trying to keep people out of this corner, which means I very definitely need to poke around. It's a shame how dusty my coat will be once I'm back outside, but costumes can always be mended, whereas secrets aren't always at leisure to be discovered. A loud blare sounds outside, and the boards shake under my boots. Only one horn of warning? Tacky. But blast it all—I'm staying. Better to be trapped in here with possibilities than trapped in Phaedro's old wagon, brooding about in the darkness and hating it.

Perhaps another man would see a grimy crypt filled with broken things, but I see endless possibilities. Sofas can be fixed. Ripped paintings can be torn from their ornate frames and replaced with, honestly, less cross-eyed bearded ladies. I push farther in, slithering around half a staircase, and something rustles up ahead. I go silent and focus my senses. If it's a person, they're using something to cloak their scent— probably the same powder I'm using to cloak mine.

"Who's there?" I bark, putting every inch of ferocity into my voice that I feel most of the time and shove down as often as necessary.

"Stain? What in the name of Aztarte are you doing in here?"

"Might as well ask you the same, love."

A shadow detaches up ahead, and the blue light dancing on my fingertips shows me Merissa's small form. She's not in her grand gowns or sweet chemise now but is clad in slim black breeches and a short cloak, her hair tucked up under a black kerchief. Washed in blue and black, she resembles a wide-eyed shadow, and I know that she's up to no good.

"I'm looking for something," she says crossly, and I grin.

"As am I. Shall we find it together?" Just for fun, I waggle my eyebrows lasciviously.

Her gloved hand flaps, dismissing me. "I suspect we're looking for different things. But the lanterns are over there, if you're still trying to illuminate your wagon. I was going to bring you one on my way. They never do give enough warning before the wagon starts."

Right before I look where she's pointing, I catch her eyes darting away and mark the spot: a trunk hastily shoved under an old rug. I think perhaps she's an accomplished liar who's unaccustomed to doubt; pretty creatures often are.

"Ah, my thoughtful, skulking girl. What are you looking for?"

"Something that belonged to Phaedro. Nothing you can find."

"This game of Twenty Questions isn't going my way, so I'll try again. How old is this caravan?"

She shrugs and edges away. "Older than me. Bailey's father ran it before him, I heard, back when each wagon was pulled by a draft horse. One of the original wheels is there, against the wall." I look where she's pointing but notice that she uses my glance to slip something into her pocket.

"Impressive," I murmur, a hand to flaking red paint on the carved spindles.

Past the wheel, way in the back, the wagon's junk takes on a distinguished sort of languor, as if it's been sitting unwanted so long that it's grown superior about it. The boxes still bear adze marks and handmade nails, and instead of lanterns, rusted candelabras tangle together in forgotten heaps. There's a smell here, a layer of magic and age that calls to me, makes me hunger for the solid feel of my grimoires and leather-bound books under my palm. I flip through a series of portraits, hand-painted posters of long-gone freaks including a lizard man, something I've never seen in person before and would literally, literally kill to have in my future show.

Merissa steps close to my back now, peering inquisitively around me.

"Grotesque," she says, and I shrug.

"Depends on which side of the velvet rope you're on, I suppose."

Beyond the paintings, a strange gleam of orange shimmers in my blue light, and I reach out to touch the faded, frayed canvas of a tent, folded neatly and crusted with age. Rummaging underneath it, I'm overcome with a vague sense of unease. Tiny hairs raise up on the back of my neck, and a chill creeps down my spine as I uncover a collection of lanterns and a single dusty brazier. I have seen these objects before. Recently. And they still seemed new then.

"Do you know anything about this?" I ask, holding my blue flame to an ancient wooden box. Inside nestle a twisted ladle, dozens of tarnished silver plates, , and a carefully folded flowered scarf.

"It's all junk," Merissa says. "From fifty years ago, when Bailey was a boy. I asked the costumer once why we never had a fortune-teller, and she went over all queer and said, *One tyromancer is enough. Never again.*" She reaches past me to hold the fire-blackened ladle up to the light. "Scrying with cheese." She shakes her head. "So primitive. So...human. I kept pushing to find a glancer, and Mrs. Cleavers told me that the elder Bailey put the fortune-teller to death. Burned her at the stake all those years ago and swore we'd never have another. Perhaps she gave a bad fortune."

"So, there's no fortune-teller in the caravan now?" I ask, an open hole filled with ice where my stomach should be.

"Of course not. Surely you noticed when you were taking stock?"

"Of course not," I echo, remembering the warmth of the light on the young girl's dark hair, the penetrative weight of her gaze. "Have you ever had your fortune told?"

Merissa shakes her head and pulls her hands away. "Wouldn't want to. It's personal, what they see. Right down to your toes, and you can't hide."

"If you've nothing to hide, it shouldn't be a problem."

"There's always something to hide. Like all this old flotsam. Don't know why someone doesn't toss everything out, or at least sell it to a scrap man on Portobello Road." She reaches for a pierced tin lamp, and I swat her hand away.

"I wanted light, and this will do. There's something to be said for objects with a purpose and a choice bit of tarnish, don't you think? An electric light can go out, but a lantern is a vessel. When the light shines through, it connects the viewer to everyone who's ever looked into the lamp, who's read a book by its light or held it up in the darkness to frighten away the monsters." I pick up the pierced lantern I remember, the one with the hooded figure surrounded by stars, forever chased by a wolf. The beeswax candle within still has a wick, and I brush the dust away, snap my fingers to light it, and close the little door. Stars and leaves dance around us, golden warm, and Merissa's honest smile is its own light. "See?"

"I do. There's a poetry to it, isn't there?"

"That there is, love."

When I offer her the lantern, she takes it, holding it high for me. The old box is heavier than it looks, but I manage to maneuver it to a clear space by the door. So, I have what I came for, light and secrets, but I'm now stuck in a moving vehicle with a woman I'd very much like to woo, which is about the loveliest situation I can think of. We have privacy, we have romantic lighting, and we have one forgotten, three-legged velvet chaise that won't suffer for a stain or two.

Tossing open the sliding door, I breathe in the afternoon sunlight. Gold fields and green trees rumble past under a leaden gray sky, and the air smells of ozone and wildflowers.

"Are you going to jump out?" Merissa asks, clutching the jamb tightly as she looks outside.

My hands find her waist and pull her back, spin her around against the wall. Ever so gently, I tip my head to kiss her, giving her every chance to pull away or push me away or say something or turn her head. But she doesn't, and I knew she wouldn't, and we're kissing and the ground is moving and I know the fortune-teller told me that I'd only get one of my desires this soon, but a woman like this is better solace than a circus.

She'll do.

By my blood and all the heavens, she'll do.

8

We're tangled up on the chaise under a filmy curtain, breathing in time together. Merissa's slender, calloused fingers trace up and down my forearm, alternately tickling and arousing. Her lovemaking is full of playful torture mixed with ferocity, and I have bruises and bite marks and absolutely no desire to move again. Ever.

"Do you love me?" she asks in a teasing voice, and I consider.

"I don't know you," I say, "But I want to."

"That's a more honest answer than most men would give, I suppose." Her wandering fingers slither over the inside of my elbow, up my bicep, over my chest. "Have you ever really loved someone before?"

I shift uncomfortably under her hands and her scrutiny. "I don't think so."

"That means no."

"Have you ever loved someone, then?"

She chuckles softly but sadly, sadly but sweetly. "Oh, I have."

"What happened to him?"

She sighs and lays her cheek against my heartbeat. "He died."

My arm curls around her, and I stroke her tumbled hair. "I'm sorry," I say, and I am.

"I'm not a brooder. I don't brood. I look to the future. I choose hope."

"That's a compelling sentiment, my girl. Choosing hope." I kiss her forehead and nuzzle her hair and wish I knew at what point infatuation became love, what sort of tender feeling made a maybe into a yes and one day into now. "But tell me. How did you know when it was love? Truly love?"

She sighs and stretches out her lithe, muscled legs, her fine-boned feet poking out the open wagon door. "I have this saying, you see. From my grandmother. *Not my circus, not my monkeys.* She would say it whenever someone brought her a problem that wasn't hers, one she didn't intend to own. If my brother pulled my pigtails or if I accidentally knocked over an inkwell, I would run to her, crying, and she would frown and shrug and say it. And so I started saying it, too, whenever a boy would court me, whenever a man would beg for my attentions. *Why won't you kiss me? Why won't you accept my proposal?*" She sighs. "Not my circus, not my monkeys."

"And so...?"

"And so, one day, with this man, I didn't say that. Not ever."

I chuckle, but I don't feel anything. "So, you found your circus and your monkeys. That's rather sweet."

"Oh, it was. But nothing stays the same, does it?"

"Change isn't always bad, love. Wouldn't you like some new monkeys?"

She turns in my arms, and her eyes dance with mischief, and she runs a claw over my lips. "Maybe I could do with one monkey. A dancing monkey. Do you dance, Stain?"

I exhale and let all my masks fall away. "I'll waltz but I'll never jig or kneel, if that's what you're asking."

Her laugh is light and lying, and I begin to wonder if every moment with Merissa is playing some sort of game, and if that's an intriguing proposition or a long, slow suicide. I want to hold her, dig my thumbs into her heart and pry it loose and hold it up to the light to see if it's made of muscle or stone or diamond. But I can't do those things, and I don't know if she would do them to me, so I do the only thing I can do.

Ever so gently, I cup her cheek and turn her face to mine and kiss us both into a stupid, lovely oblivion.

THE TRAIN STOPS at dusk, and Merissa hops down first and scurries away, muttering about seeing to the horses. I'm gratified to note that her usual, practiced, swaying walk is more than a little bow-legged. Whoever her last monkey was, he clearly didn't have my skills and stamina.

When I leave, I take the box with me. A few whispered words and a dash of powder sprinkled on my head and the eyes of the milling, laughing carnivalleros skitter over me like a crack in fine porcelain. I don't want to talk to anyone. As pleasant a diversion and as intriguing a future as Merissa might present, I haven't been able to stop thinking about how I had my fortune told by a ghost in a caravan with no fortune-teller. The answers, I know, are under the orange cloth in this box.

My wagon is still dark, but something is off. Someone has been here since I left. I can't smell their mark or see anything missing, but the back of my neck prickles and I can't rest until I've checked every hiding place. Once the new lanterns are spread about, the entire space takes on an eerie, honey-warm glow. The pierced lantern is the last one I light, and I place it in the center of the room, on a spindly table, and rotate it so that the girl and the wolf are on opposite walls. I think I might smell the faintest, nutty hint of cheese, and I follow the scent to a corner where the wallpaper is peeling. I tug down the hideous purple, a lower layer of flowers, a layer of sepia-toned newspaper, and reveal...warm orange.

"This was your wagon, wasn't it?" I whisper to the still air, and the lantern spins of its own accord as if held in a small girl's hand, the stars whirling dizzily. I lift out the next layer of possessions in the old box. Dozens of dishes, porcelain and tin, each one lovingly clean but old enough to show the marks of an artisan's hands, unlike today's factory-produced rubbish. About fifty silver knives fall out when I unroll the flowered scarf. It reminds me of the one my mother used to keep her tarot cards in, and I hold it up to the light and trace the silk roses and vines with a sigh of nostalgia.

The box is almost empty now, just scraps of old newspaper and a mending kit for the tent. I marvel over the rolled, stitched leather, running my fingers over the bone needles and slubby thread and tiny thimbles. Did the little girl live alone? How did she set up such a large tent by herself? Where was her family? How did she come to be a—what had Merissa called it? A tyromancer.

At what point does one wake up and decide to seek the future in runny cheese?

There's a lump in the mending kit, and I fish out a tarnished chain and locket. There's a setting for a jewel on one side, but whatever past frippery it once held is long gone. On the other side is a compass rose. When I flick open the clasp, I find a portrait inside. It's a beautiful woman with riotous black hair, her chin up and her dark blue eyes firm. Something about her seems to challenge me in a way that makes one of my eyebrows raise automatically. Could it be the little girl as a grown woman? Not if Bailey murdered her young. Her mother, perhaps? But the woman's clothing is modern, her hat of a style I haven't seen before. So who is she? Under the woman's portrait is the name Letitia, written in my own handwriting, and if I wasn't unsettled before, I tell you I am now.

"The locket will draw her to you."

It's the little girl's voice, coming from nowhere and everywhere. And I know that she's dead, that old Bailey had her burned at the stake, but I feel like she's here in the room with me, wrapped in the warm scent of beeswax and cheese and the comfort of an unforeseen future.

My head swims, and I could swear I hear her laughing. The lights flicker, and the pierced lantern spins in a wind that definitely isn't there, sending stars and wolf teeth dancing across the dark walls, faster and faster. Something rustles in the far side of the wagon, and I hunch over, fingers curling into claws.

"Who's there?" I growl.

No one answers, but I'm not alone, not really. The little girl's words echo in my mind: *Magic, time, tenacity, sacrifice. The locket will draw her to you.* I have all five things but no idea how to apply them. Is this what will secure my future caravan? Because I have Merissa, my ruby beauty, and the lady from the portrait isn't even a Bludwoman. She's human.

It doesn't matter now—I'm hunting. I drop the locket and chain in my breast pocket, pocket number one, and stand. As I stalk through the field of spinning stars,, I draw my claws over the wallpaper, not minding that I'm scoring it, hoping to reach the cozy orange at the bottom. Something rustles again, furtive, towards the back of the wagon, where the bed is. I can walk silently when I wish it, and so I do, because if whatever has intruded on my privacy is killable, I'm going to kill it.

This corner of the room is silent and dark, untouched by the lanterns' warmth. Tall armoires and knobby tables loom, cutting the space into a million shadows. I drop to hands and knees and sniff the ground for some sign of trespass. Silence builds, like the ghost is waiting, worried, like maybe I'm not the most dangerous thing in the room. There's a scrape under the bed, and I dive for it, my talons raking the wooden boards and clutching...nothing.

Air from an open trapdoor.

I knock the bed over and hunt for clues, but there's no odor, no hair, no nothing. Whoever has been here must use the same powder I do to mask their scent. I'm too smart to stick my head out; I'll investigate from outside with weapons in hand once I've secured my home. Growling, I yank the door closed and latch it. For good measure, I right the bed, shove it to the other side of the room, and drag a heavy armoire over to completely cover the escape hatch cut into my floor. The only person in this caravan who should be able to budge it from below is the strong lady, and her shoulders wouldn't even fit through the hole. But someone has been here, and I know neither why nor whom.

A harsh knock on the door startles me out of my furious befuddlement.

"What?" I roar.

"Thought you might like some dinner, but not if it gets my head bitten off," Merissa calls through the door, but I can tell she's at least vaguely amused.

We are predators, after all, and a predator defends its den to the death.

"Just a moment, love," I yell, stepping before the mirror to clean off the dust I'm sure I accumulated poking around, literally and euphemistically, in the prop wagon.

The mirror is a heavy, old-fashioned thing in an ornate oval frame, set into the typical wagon faucet and ewer. We're not tapped into the aquifer yet, most likely, but there's enough water in the sink to wipe off the grime. When I look up, I see the little girl's face as if through a clear pond.

"Whatever she gives you, don't take it," she whispers.

When I blink, she's gone.

"Bloody ghosts," I mutter, deeply troubled and with every hair on my body standing at attention. I whip out the locket, but the portrait is gone, the tarnished metal clips cradling nothing. "Bloody disappearing ghost women!"

"Stain? Who're you talking to?"

I make a play of laughing as I swagger to the door, but I'm shaken to the core. Did I imagine the portrait? And the ghost? Am I going mad? No matter; I've known plenty of mad people, and they seem to get along fine. But still…the world is off kilter, and I'd like to find my footing.

I toss open the door and grin. "Just talking to myself, lass. Best company there is."

She laughs with me, but it doesn't reach her eyes as she peers around me into the darkness. "You're leaving the lamps on?"

"Ah, no. Just a moment." I hurry around the room, blowing out the lights until nothing is left but the buzzing of the electrics, and it reminds me of an animal almost dead that won't quite die.

Once we're outside, I let my handkerchief drop so I have reason to kneel and peer under the wagon, but there's no sign of my intruder or any damage. When I stand, she takes my hand, our fingers laced together and swinging.

It's a beautiful evening after a strange, beautiful day, and the caravan is drenched in the pink light of a lazy sunset. Laughter rides the breeze, leaking out the open door and windows of the dining car. We'll set up the caravan tomorrow morning and perform until dawn tomorrow night, but for now, the carnivalleros can rest and relax after a long day of traveling. Two hungry bludbunnies lurk at the step, trying their damnedest to bypass biology and learn how to take the stairs. Merissa and I stoop in tandem, snatch them up by the ears, and knock them out against the corner before hanging them from the waiting meat hooks. It's my first time adding meat to the human's food supply in Bailey's caravan, and Merissa writes my name in chalk on the blackboard next to my first hash mark.

STAIN, it says.

She's never called me Criminy, and I long to hear it on her lush lips.

I've never known her last name, and I wish to whisper it into my pillow.

Up the stairs and into the wagon we go, and I've never seen it so crowded. Dozens of humans, daimons, freaks, and a precious few Bludmen crowd the space, jostling for their favorite tidbits and seats.

"Find us a bench, will you, Stain?" Merissa flaps a hand at me, and I give her a small bow and head for the black-painted corner. Catarrh and Quincy are there, as well as the hawkish old costumer, a beautiful blonde woman with red-painted lips, and a mournful sort of fellow with auburn hair.

I pause, unsure of the best way to make friends rather than enemies, and Merissa appears at my side and inclines her head towards a space on the bench.

"Folk, this is Mr. Stain, our new magician. Stain, this is Mrs. Cleavers, the costumer; Charlie Dregs, the puppet master, and Tabitha Scowl, occasional mermaid and part-time bearded lady."

"Pretend bearded lady," the blonde woman says, her eyes skimming me hungrily, and she does look rather nice without the fake beard.

I smile and shake hands and mutter politenesses, and as I settle my coattails and sit again, Merissa slides a teacup of blood in front of me. "And you know Catarrh and Quincy, naturally."

"Naturally," I say, swirling my blood around as I consider.

Because here is the question: When a ghost tells you not to drink something, do you drink it?

Merissa nudges my elbow. "Drink, silly," she says, and I decide I damn well won't.

"Pardon me just a moment, pet." I scoot out of the bench like a greased weasel and head for the drink buffet, where Laraby is pouring himself a colorful daimon brew and laughing with Mademoiselle Caprice.

"You're looking blue, my friend," I say, smacking him on the back in the way of strong males being friendly.

"Had a bit of help there," he says, grinning. His skin is at least four shades more brilliant than the last time I saw him, and he seems a far more cheerful fellow. "Well done with Phaedro, by the by. Quite a show there."

"Just goes to prove I make a far better friend than an enemy." With my back to the room, I select a vial from the cauldron, pop the cork, and guzzle it in a few gulps.

"My, my, monsieur. Impatient, are we?" Mademoiselle Caprice says.

I snatch another vial and down it, too. "A long day's travel makes a fellow thirsty, ma chère." But her knowing smile tells me her finely attuned daimon senses know exactly what I've been up to. She most likely feeds on lust in addition to the crowd's applause. With a wink and a smile, I slip the empty vials into my coat and return to my table.

"What was that all about?" Merissa asks.

"I helped Laraby with his act and wanted to hear how he was getting along."

"Daimons and Bludmen? Disgusting," Catarrh says.

"Something tells me they think the same thing about you lads."

Quincy hisses at me, and Catarrh knocks his head against his brother's in warning.

"Drink your blood before it gets cold, dear," Merissa says sweetly.

For possibly the first time in my life, a cup of blood strikes me as utterly unappetizing. It's fresh enough, but that doesn't matter. Whether it's safe or not, whether it's cold or warm, I'm not touching that teacup. Instead, I knock it over with my elbow while reaching for Merissa's hand.

She squeals and surges out of the booth before the murky red gunk can splatter her green dress. "Never considered you clumsy," she says, and she sounds like a scolding nursemaid.

"Yes, well, it's been a rather challenging week, my love. Duels to the death and such." My most devoted, eyelash-batting gaze only serves to infuriate her, but she reins it in and stuffs her frustration into a tight and brittle smile.

"Let me get you another cup then, darling."

"Oh, but that wouldn't be gentlemanly, poppet." I stand, sidestep the blood, and swing her around to sit beside Tabitha at the other, clean table. "Do allow me to tidy up my own mess. I'll bring you another cup, shall I?" And before she can splutter an answer, I'm headed for the cook's window for an old towel, wondering what the hell she's about.

When I turn back holding two teacups, two vials, and a rag, she's gone, and Tabitha is laughing so hard, she's puce.

"Women," Catarrh says with a disgusted shake of his head.

"You shouldn't blame women for Merissa's behavior any more than women should blame men in general for yours, you cheating, murdering sociopath," I say, mopping up the blood.

Because this is not a lovers' spat. This is me being strange because ghosts are ordering me about. And Merissa being strange because she's up to no good.

9

I sleep alone, wrapped in uncertainty. Whether or not she intends me harm, I would still prefer to be wrapped up in Merissa. What relationship ever bloomed without some secret, some dangerous games? We are, after all, Bludmen. Apex predators, tigers in tailcoats and cougars in corsets. I never asked for complete honesty, but I'm also not enthusiastic about having mysterious things dropped in my drink.

I don't chase her, nor does she seek me out.

The ghost doesn't make another appearance, but I find I'm very glad I overpaid her.

In short, nothing happens, and then it is morning.

Setup day around the caravan is both very similar and very different wherever one goes, and I cheerfully take part in the process. Casca, the strong lady, is glad for my help sinking the poles for the tightrope walker, considering the old man isn't strong enough to heft his own timbers. His little granddaughters watch patiently, and the moment the wire rope is ready, they scamper straight up to practice their arabesques while he pretends to take his rest with a snifter of whisky.

The freaks are glad for both my magic and my muscles as they set up their tent, and I learn quickly how to pull the stage down from my own wagon's wall. It's hollow, and Phaedro had packed it to the gills with trapdoors, tricks, and traps. As I paw through his old trunks, an excitable child arrives to watch me, buzzing like a bumblebee in ill-fitting clothes and an aviator's cap, and carrying a ladder and a tool bag large enough for him to sleep in.

"Need something, lad?" I ask, not exactly unpleasantly, but in a way that says I'm not on duty as an act yet and won't stand for quite so much staring.

"I'm here to paint your wagon, sir," he says, holding up two pots of paint.

I nod and smile. "You're a bit young, aren't you?"

"My name is Vil, sir, and I've the steadiest hand outside of London. Do the odd jobs for Master Bailey, you see." With both hands and a grunt, he hefts his leather bag and drops it with a clank.

"Go on, then." He leans the ladder against the wagon and quickly sets to work with his brushes and far more concentration than I expected of one so young. "Tell me, Vil. You ever seen Master Bailey?"

"No, sir. No one has. Not in ten years gone. But we get paid regular through his window and no one gets beaten, which tells me it's much better here than elsewhere."

We lapse into a professional silence as he works, and I go back to rummaging through Phaedro's trunks. All the best things I'd hoped to find are gone. No grimoires, no potions and powders to keep my stores healthy. A proper magician should have a cabinet of supplies, but all I find are props, cheap tricks, and clever illusions—nothing of substance.

"Bugger," I growl to myself, knowing there must be something more.

"You don't like the color, sir?"

My annoyance fades when I look up. "No, lad. The color's fine. Looks much better with Phaedro's name painted out."

With a sigh of relief, the boy clambers down from his perch with his pot of paint in hand and wet brush in his mouth. Without asking for any help, he tugs his ladder to the other end of the wagon and starts a series of glorious curlicues that magically connect into my name. Pride rushes into me, and I allow myself a grin before tamping it back down again. It doesn't pay to look cocky when contemplating a hostile takeover.

"What else should it say, sir?"

I look up. *Criminy the Great* scrolls across the wagon in a shower of stars.

"It's perfect, lad," I say. And it is.

For now.

I'll be a little more explicit when I have him repaint Bailey's wagon for me.

At lunch, I venture to the other side of the dining car and move among the carnivalleros. A few of the more skittish humans shudder when I touch their shoulders and look directly into their eyes, but soon, I've got them all smiling, laughing, divulging their secrets. Casca needs better weights; one of the freak tents is so worn through that people are getting a free show. The flea circus lady heard there was a traveling apothecary who kept an entire wagon filled with jars of wonders and terrors, and for the right price, he might let it go. And I agree that we must acquire it.

A master must never forget that listening is his best weapon. People who feel they aren't heard start to yell, and then it's a lot harder to shut their mouths and open their hearts. Bailey's been hiding too long, and his speakerphone is a one-way street. I mentally catalog their grievances, tie them to faces and names and acts and wagons. This little kingdom is so very in need of a king.

All I have to do is kill the old king.

But first, I owe a visit to my prospective queen.

With enthusiastic goodbyes, I leave the dining wagon, fairly sure I've made many friends and the requisite few enemies. Those who hunger for ambition always do, and it does keep me on my toes. I scroll through my mental list of what needs doing around the caravan, aching for a pen and paper and fairly certain that when I'm in charge, Vil will serve as my secretary.

Merissa's wagon is open, a pile of manure and straw by the wide door on the horses' side. Kali and Fausta are picketed in the field, each dining on what looks like half of a pig's carcass, crunching the bones with their huge, flat teeth. I pat their elegant necks, admire their gleaming coats. The scent of blood draws me closer to the open section of Merissa's car, and I find the rest of the carcass hanging from a hook, the skin stripped off. The smell is pleasant, and I'm curious what cultivated flesh tastes like, but there's barely any blood left, and it won't win Merissa back by stealing from her pets.

"Stain? What are you doing?"

Oh, but she's beautiful when she's angry, hands on her hips and fine curves clad in a gentleman's work clothes, ratty and blood-stained. Her hair is in a long braid, her sleeves rolled up to her elbows. I want to throw her in the straw and take her right here, right now, with the door open and the meat perfuming the air.

"Looking for you, love. Although Kali and Fausta are looking handsome today."

She rolls her eyes. "They're handsome every day. You found me. Get out of my wagon and tell me what you want."

I hop down lightly and curl my hands around her waist, leaning in to nip at her lips. She goes stiff for a moment, then melts into my kiss. I take my time before pulling away to guide a stray lock of hair behind her deliciously elfin ear. "Darling, I love you when you're imperious and cruel. But I wanted to enlist your help. Unless you'd care to muss your hair a bit more?" I jerk my chin at the wagon and quirk an eyebrow.

She shoves me away roughly, but the kind of rough that makes a man's heart beat faster. "I've no time for this, Stain. I've work to do. As do you. Are you ready for your act tonight? Have you practiced? Do you need assistants? You'll have to negotiate with Tess if you want to cut her in half, you know. She's well aware of her value."

I grin and shrug. "There's time. And I don't play with party tricks. My magic is real."

"Oh, and Phaedro's wasn't?"

"Not from what I've seen in his props. But perhaps you knew him more...intimately?"

It tugs at me, how I remember Phaedro watching her as she worked her horses, how she stood so close to the stage on the night we dueled and tried to stop me with her whip. She's biting her lip now, pulling away from my hot hands and turning to touch Fausta like the horse is her only lifeline and she's drowning. I want her to touch me like that, too. I step close behind her, and she lets me wrap my arms around her. When my lips land on her neck, she quivers and twitches out of my grasp. It's a strange dance that I'm not sure yet how to follow, the way she pushes and pulls me, yet I only want her more.

"Ah, the Great Stain. You think you know everything, but you know nothing of this place. Every caravan is a different world, and every person within it their own universe. So, play house in your new wagon and craft your new act and try to find your place, but don't throw the past in my face again."

"Or else what, my lovely philosopher?" I ask, all silky smooth, because I'm not one for taking orders, not even from women I want to love.

She whips around to face me, and her braid snaps in the breeze, and she's the most ferocious little creature I've ever seen, and I almost, almost want to worship at her feet. "Or else you'll lose your place entirely. The caravan takes care of its own."

It's an old adage, and one I fully support, unless it means I'm the one who's tossed to the moors and never found again. But I suppose she's right. I do want to find my place. And my place is in Bailey's wagon, breathing new life into this broken-down catastrophe of a circus. I'll show her an act she'll never forget.

"As you wish, my lady." I give her a bow that she ignores and return to my wagon to plan my next move.

It's almost time to rehearse my show, and I'm brushing my hair by candlelight in a very masculine manner when I first smell smoke. It's a warm day, which means the ashes in my own fireplace are cold. I drop the brush and spin, hunting for flames. They're easy to find. My closed door is on fire.

My ewer is empty, and when I turn the faucet, nothing comes out. Which either means I was never connected to the aquifer or someone was rather invested in me not having enough water available to put out the fire that's devouring my only door. With a growl, I snatch the coverlet off my bed and hurry to smother the fire before it spreads.

It doesn't work. The flames lick at my coat, and I back away, the beast inside me recognizing one of the very few things a Bludman must fear. I can live to be three hundred, I can go days without drinking blood, I can turn soft, easily broken humans into strong, fast-healing Bludmen like myself. But fire will burn me as easily as paper, and the door is a wall of flame.

The air is going bad and thick and heavy, and I tuck my family grimoire into the back of my trousers, drop to my hands and knees, and crawl like a dog to the opposite end of the wagon, where the trapdoor waits. I push over the armoire with one hand and tug at the clasp, but the damned thing won't open. No matter how hard I pound with my fists or my boots, the door is surely stuck. Even close to the floor, the air is unbreathable, and I run claws along the seams of the boards, all the way to the wall. Phaedro was a magician; there must be another trapdoor, a hidden wall, a loose board—anything that will get me out of this conflagrating tomb.

The crackling builds as I tear the wallpaper with my claws and find only more wallpaper, all the way down to the orange. I dash the bed to bits against the heavy wall and hurl an empty trunk across the room, but these old wagons are built to last. My eyes sting and it's hard to see now, and more than the door must've caught. But no one is screaming on the other side of the wall, and no one is hacking into the wood with an axe to save me, and if I don't find a way out, no one will suffer for doing this to me.

Because it can't be an accident.

Doors don't catch fire on their own.

And trapdoors don't magically seal themselves from the outside.

That's what drives me, keeps pushing me to fight. I look up at the ceiling, hands in fists to scream my rage, and that's when I see it.

Ah, yes. Of course.

There's a square cut into the ceiling with a hatch.

A hatch that I can't reach.

I pull a table over, pile on a trunk, balance a chair, and shimmy up. My work with the acrobats has paid off. The air is no clearer up here, and I couch as I unclasp the door and push it open on a bright blue afternoon that smells like hope and revenge. With a heavy kick, I push up to my waist and crawl out onto the wagon's curved top. I drop my grimoire with a thump and flop over on my back, inhaling deeply. The sky above is clear and fine. Even the smoke billowing from my trailer is picturesque.

When I stand and look down, I see nothing. No crowd, no bucket brigade. The caravan is eerily silent. Judging by the sun, they're likely in the dining wagon for dinner, damn them.

I count the cars to a bright red one. Master Bailey's car.

There are no witnesses, and everything I own is on fire, on this roof, or in the jacket on my back.

Might as well get on with it. The tyromancer said decades, but maybe she was being pessimistic.

10

With a running leap, I land on the next wagon. A few strides later, and I'm on the third. Before a minute has passed, I'm on the wagon before Master Bailey's, a grass-green one that's seen better days. I'm not even breathing heavily, but I'm lit from within, as if the flames someone set to my door crawled into my heart.

A caravan where people go around setting each other on fire needs a firmer master.

Bailey's wagon is the biggest, naturally, with a windowed cupola on top. The brass clasp on the side of the biggest window suggests I can pop it open and climb inside. I do a final check of the weapons in my coat: powders, potions, poisons, a garrote. I've never seen this Bailey fellow, and so I have no idea how to best him. I can only hope that a man so frightened of the world that he never goes outside—well, I'm hoping he's a great aged slug without much fight left in him.

Maybe it's a bit underhanded, but I'm beyond morality at this point, and I've already admitted I don't fight fair. I pull a small bag out of pocket thirty-one and sprinkle some ash-like powder on the soles of my boots and the palms of my hands. When I leap onto Bailey's trailer, there is utterly no sound. With a few drops of oil, no telltale squeal of a window's latch breaks the silence. Thanks to the powder, the loudest noise I'm making is the hammering of my heart, the beating of my pulse urging me down into the dark, stuffy stillness of the caravan master's inner sanctum.

Instead of wasting my time on the rungs, I leap lightly to the ground and land in a crouch, the grimoire held in my hand like a club. The wagon is dark and cluttered, and the smell is well-nigh unbearable. The stale reek of unbathed human flesh hangs heavily over the more welcome scent of old paper and tobacco, and underneath it all lurks the deep, wet rot of abandoned human food. I can smell past fires, heaps of coppers, perhaps the tang of a dog long gone. The man must live like a doomed dragon, winding among these heaps of refuse, towering piles of paper, boxes of hoarded coins, and a minefield of spittoons.

And yet...I don't smell a living human, as I did when visiting his window twice before.

Just an overabundance of a human's blood, fresh and insistent.

Which isn't quite right.

Something creaks, and I hear whispered voices.

The first is raspy and rough and low. "I need more."

"I brought it. Here. Take mine, too. Does it hurt much?"

My heart shatters when I recognize Merissa's whisper. There's a sweetness, a worry, a vulnerability that I've never heard from her, and disgust floods me. I thought her a haughty equal, but if she's in love with a filthy, cowardly human, I obviously was deeply wrong. No wonder she wouldn't help me take over the caravan, if she's secretly in love with Master Bailey.

I creep closer on silent, enchanted feet. The scent of warm blood dominates the air, and I salivate and have to wipe my lip. As my eyes adjust, I see a lump on a bed, huddled under blankets by the light of a banked fire. Potion bottles and herb packets and powders are scattered around the floor, all of the magic supplies I've been hunting since I took over my wagon. A bucket filled with wet red and pink meat sits by the bed, and I think I see intestines and a finger in the puddled muck.

Merissa is wrapped in a dark cloak, putting a steaming cup into clammy white hands and guiding them towards the figure. Is she feeding Bailey blood? Is that why he hides in his wagon, so his employees won't know he's become a predator like us?

This scene…makes no sense.

"Is it working?" she asks with a frown, the back of her hand to his brow.

The blanketed figure resettles. "Yes. But it hurts."

"My poor love." She leans forwards to embrace him, and he sighs in contentment, and I want to rip out his heart with my claws.

"Did you take care of him?" the figure asks. The voice is nothing like what I remember through the speaker, but that's the whole point of a speaker, isn't it? He sounds broken, all gargles and burbles.

Merissa waits until he's done coughing and gives a ravishing smile. "It's done. And they haven't even left the dining car yet. The wagon will be a pile of cinders by showtime."

"I hate to lose a wagon…"

She shakes her head. "Sometimes, you throw the baby out with the bathwater, darling. It's better this way. I couldn't stand the way he touched me." When Merissa shivers in disgust, I grow cold. To think I brought her love and intimacy, and she tried to immolate me in my own home. I'm a little impressed and mostly hateful, and I finally understand why my mother once told me, "Love lies, but so does fear."

The tyromancer was wrong. It's not love that comes with ruby-red blood in the forest; it's death. A boy's infatuation almost got me killed.

"Is there more?" he asks.

Merissa laughs fondly. "It's your caravan. You can have all the blood you want, can't you?"

"Hurry back," he says, settling into his pillows as she leaves by the front door.

And that's my cue.

Time to take what's mine.

11

stalk through the wagon to loom over the bed, but I'm just as surprised as he is when I get there.

"I already killed you," I say.

The Great Phaedro coughs a laugh. "Then you didn't do a very good job."

"You look rather dead." I drop my book, cross my arms, and eye him.

He's not so great anymore, not that he was great to begin with. He looks like a corpse, waxy white with purple hollows under his eyes and cheeks and bloody spittle caked around his lips. A woolly scarf wraps around his neck, and the rest of him is a mound of blankets, skeletal white hands clutching a teacup of clotting blood over his stomach. He doesn't seem scared of me, which is a good sign that he's hiding something. Whether it's a weapon or a defense, I can't be sure. So, I do what any murderous monster would do at a time like this: I claw for his eyes.

His flesh parts like mud under my talons, an unsettling feeling that my body responds to with a second slash across his cheek. Bony fingers catch my wrist, hard as a manacle, and a death rattle of a laugh bubbles up out of whatever has become of Phaedro.

"If ripping out my throat didn't work, did you really think blinding me would? Fool."

As I watch, his flesh begins to knit. Not like normal skin, with pink edges and scabs and blood, because there is no blood. It pulls together with a sick squelch, as vile as the congress of slugs. The eye I destroyed shifts and puddles like black ink, and Phaedro laughs with the shriveled mouth of a corpse.

"A few more bodies' worth of blood and meat, and you won't be able to tell the difference," he says, waving his other hand at the bucket of intestines. "I'm thus improved after draining and eating half of old Bailey, and he was practically a dead man before that. I'm thinking the little Fetchings girls would be delicious, don't you?"

I pull away, disgusted. "The tightrope walker's granddaughters? That's monstrous." I think of how tiny and bird-boned and innocent they are, dancing fearlessly like sparrows on their wire, and the blood rises in my gorge. "I'm a monster, but I'm not that kind of monster."

"There's only one kind of monster, Stain. And you clearly know nothing of necromancy. The purer the sacrifice, the farther it goes. If I ever want to look alive again, I'm going to need lots of young, fresh meat."

Anger bubbles up, and with it, my beast. The dark room washes over in red, and I howl and lunge for his face with my claws, scoring his forehead in parallel slashes and ripping open one cheek. He starts whispering a spell, and I grab the scarf wrapped around his throat and shove the end of it down his throat. His body jerks, his hands scrabbling to clear his mouth, and I grab them, one by one, and snap his wrists as easily as kindling. It's like fighting a possessed doll that shouldn't be moving in the first place, unnatural and floppy and yet so persistently determined to keep slapping me away. He's bucking under me, silently screaming around the scarf, flailing with snapped hands and fingers that can't quite grab me.

Straddling him with a knee on each dancing arm, I unwind the other end of his scarf to find a grotesquely half-healed crevasse where his throat should be. The tubes have grown back roughly, weaving around in front of his spine, but the skin hasn't quite made it back across. I reach into the wet, red-black mess, grab a tangle of veins and whatever the hell else makes up a man, and yank them out like I'm shutting down an automaton.

He just laughs.

Breathless, eyes black pits, broken and wet and flopping—he laughs.

I'm yanking off his lips when the door flies open and Merissa shrieks like a demon straight out of hell.

"What are you doing? What have you done? You bastard!"

She's so lovely in her wrath that I almost forget that she'll kill me if she can. The same instinct that made me go for Phaedro's eyes has her claws arcing towards my face, and I snatch her fine wrists in both hands and want to laugh at how very breakable people are. She grunts and tries to yank away from me, tries to kick me, but she's after all just a tiny thing and can't even come close. The only part of me she ever hurt was my heart, and she can't reach that anymore.

"You've been a very naughty girl," I say. "You set out to capture more than just a horse that morning, didn't you?"

The fight goes out of her, or she wants me to think it does. Her arms go to her sides, her hair falling over her face as she sighs like the wind in blood-spattered branches.

"No. I just needed another horse for my act and I'd heard there was a white one nearby."

"Who told you?"

If I wasn't watching her face so closely, I might've missed the fear that flashed in the green, glowing depths of her eyes.

"You know who told me. The tyromancer. She comes to everyone on their first day here. Told me I would get what I'd always wanted if I followed a rainbow to a birch forest and caught a white horse."

"What you'd always wanted, eh? And to think you threw me away," I say, bitterness dripping.

"It was never you, you idiot." She tosses back her head and laughs, cutting me deep. "It was Phaedro. We've been planning it for weeks, but the timeline changed when you showed up and got in the way. Necromancy requires bodies, and it was past time for Bailey to disappear. All I wanted was to rule this caravan with Phaedro. And I did get it. For almost an entire day."

She leans around me, yanks a hand away to touch his ruined throat.

"We can have it again, darling," she whispers. "All is not lost."

I step away, cold as ice and twice as hard. "You're mad as a hatter, love."

Merissa whirls on me, hands up in claws. "You wouldn't know love if it called you by name, Stain." I take a step back, and she presses forwards. "And what will you do with me, eh? Chain me to your bed? Kill me and doom him? Hold us prisoner in this wretched boxcar of death?"

I step out of striking range and can't help but laugh. "Look, lass. I've no use for an unwilling woman. Take your carcass of a necromancer and your matched white horses and go where you will." She cocks her head at me and smiles as if I'm a stupid child, and I draw power and will around me like a cloak. "But do not make the mistake of assuming me soft and merciful. If I ever see either of you again, if you ever make a move against me or my caravan, I will destroy you both. For good."

"You're letting us go?" She steps back dumbly and sits on the edge of the bed. Phaedro's ruined hand flops around towards her, and she takes it gently between both of her own and rubs the shattered bones tenderly.

"It's all I wanted, really." I shrug. "This caravan. Thought I wanted to rule it with you, but this'll do."

"You're a very strange man, Criminy Stain."

"I'm not a man. I'm a ringmaster. Now get the hell out of my circus, and take your broken monkey with you."

12

They've disappeared before the stage lights go up, but no one seems to know any difference. The caravan has run like a rusty machine for so long that the show plays on as usual without Merissa and her Mesmerizing Mares. I simply close the doors on her wagon, and the audience ignores the empty spot and hurries on to the next lively show.

As for me, my stage has burned to the ground, my wagon now but a smoldering pile of timbers. Instead of drawing my own crowd, I wander among the flow of bodies, doing small shows and finding refuge, as ever, among the humans I consider so far below me. Their amazement, their wonder, their joy, their occasional unwarranted terror. Instead of choosing a girl in bloom, as I'd always done, I present flowers to an old maid in the crowd, making her withered cheeks blush. This time, there is no price tag on the gift, no taste or threat of the future.

I'm done with making women disappear.

THE NEXT MORNING at breakfast, I walk into the dining car with Vil by my side, a notebook and pen in his hands and a smile on my face.

"Listen up, you lot," I say in an ever-so-slightly charmed voice that requires no speakerphone. "Master Bailey is dead. Merissa killed him and ran off. You can find his remains hanging in her wagon, if you wish." The whispering starts, and I hush it with a hand. "I'm taking over this caravan. I know how to run it, and you'll find me a fair master. Everyone's equal: Bludman, human, daimon, other, male, female, whatever. Everyone gets a raise, starting tonight—double what Bailey paid you. And I want to hear your ideas for improving the show as a whole. I'll not hide behind a closed door and a speaker. I'll help you raise the poles and chop the wood, and I'll defend each of you, if you stay, with my life." I cross my arms and drop my chin, pulling the mantle of a Bludman's beast around me. "But if anyone—anyone—wishes to challenge me, fight me, sabotage me, or hurt me or any of mine, I assure you right now that you will die in a messier manner than Phaedro the Great. Any questions?"

The carnivalleros are weirdly silent...aside from the two youngest ones. The Fetchings girls are whispering fiercely, and the smaller one pushes the older one forwards through the crowd. She squeezes out in front of me in her slightly too-small, altogether too-bright costume.

"The name's Emerlie Fetchings, sir. Found this sitting in the ashes of your old trailer this morning." With trembling hands, she puts the familiar lamp on the floor at my feet, as if she's afraid of touching me. "Everything else was burnt to a crisp, but it was sittin' there, proud as you like. Thought you might want it."

I pick it up, expecting it to be hot to the touch. But the pierced metal is as cool as ever, unmarred by fire or smoke, although the candle stub within has melted cleanly away.

The letter L is carved into the plate where a candle has always sat, and understanding and weirdness flood through me.

I have everything I want now but one thing, and the tyromancer promised me I would have that, too, one day. I had thought Merissa was mine, that she was my ruby-bedecked love, unafraid among the birches. She wasn't, and I should have known it, and she's gone forever, a younger man's folly. And now that it turns out the caravan was on the shorter time frame, that means I have decades still to wait for my true love. And her name will be Letitia. And she will have dark, tumbling hair and fine blue eyes that match a portrait that only existed for a heartbeat in an old, broken locket given to me by a ghost in a wagon that's now ashes.

My new quest is to figure out how to bring her here, to the hard-won circus that fulfills half my destiny. How to fix this locket and charm it and send it to draw her to me, as the tyromancer bade me do. If I can solve this puzzle, then perhaps one day I'll find myself in another forest of stark black and white trees, but this time I'll find my heart's desire.

My hand goes to my breast pocket, where the necklace sits heavy and strangely warm, and I do wonder if we'll be haunted all our days by a serious, dark-eyed little girl in a mysterious orange tent that only appears to welcome newcomers to the caravan. Or perhaps the tent and her memory burned down with my wagon, with the spoon and the knives and the brazier. Perhaps it's time for this circus to find a new fortune-teller to go with its new fortune.

I shake off the fancy. There's work to be done, and now.

"Good job, lass," I say, pulling a copper from behind Emerlie's cropped golden curls.

She snatches it with a gap-toothed grin but doesn't back away or flinch, which tells me she's going to be a pain for the rest of our days together, the bright little sparrow hawk.

"Also, sir, while you're in a good mood…I'd like a wagon of me own."

I chuckle and shake my head. "Not my circus, not my monkeys. In a few decades, maybe, once you're a star. Once you've earned it. Until then, let's get back to business, shall we?"

They file out the door, murmuring excitedly about the prospect of a raise, and I'm left in the dining car with no one but Vil.

"What's your first order, sir?" he asks, quill poised.

"Repaint the tables and benches in here so that they're all the same color," I say.

He nods and scribbles. "Do I do that before I repaint your wagon?"

I put a hand on his shoulder, throw back my head, and laugh. "You'll get a raise, too, lad. Paint *Criminy's Captivating Caravan* on Bailey's old wagon and get ready to burn most of his old things."

"What next?"

I look around, mind spinning. "Sit down, lad. It's going to be a long list."

When I step outside of my new wagon at dusk, I'm rewarded with the loveliest view: an enormous crowd of humans waiting at the turnstile.

"Who collects the admission?" I ask Vil.

He doesn't even pause in his painting. "Whoever you wish, sir," he answers, adding stars around the Y in my name.

And tonight, for now, it will be me. I retie my cravat and settle my hat as I stride the beaten path to where the audience waits, barely breathing, for the excitement we alone can provide.

This is my circus, and these are my monkeys, but still, I am hungry for more.

INTERLUDE: SWALLOW

A MIRIAM BLACK NOVELLA

CHUCK WENDIG

1

Now: The Bird Doctor Is In

An ungracious breath of air, a grunt, and Miriam's eyes jolt open. Her face, tacky with saliva. Her skull pounds like a bouncy house full of rowdy kids. She pulls her face away from a pillow. Doesn't know how she got here. Doesn't even know where the fuck she is.

Room's dark. She sits up. Tries not to make a sound.

Ahead: a rectangle of darkness lighter than the shadows around her. Gray, not black. A faint liquid shine to it—moonlight, starlight, something.

A window.

She feels her head. A light crusting of blood. Granular, flaky, like the charred end of a steak left too long on the grill.

Her tongue tastes blood, too. Inside her mouth: a stinging pain. A cut on the inside of her cheek.

Her neck hurts, too. There her finger probes, finds a small wound.

A tranquilizer dart. She remembers coming up to the house, opening the door—something striking her in the neck. Then the world going topsy-turvy.

Her brain tries to catch up to her predicament. *I came here. Where is this? Why did I come here? Shit, shit, shit. Think, dum-dum. Think!*

Everything, a cloud. Thinking right now is like running in mud.

She stands. Bedsprings squeak. Her foot hits the floor and that squeaks, too, and suddenly she's thinking, *I'm making too much noise,* and a whip of fear lashes back, catches her right on the chin, and suddenly she's worried about alerting—who? Someone. Her stomach falls out like a broken elevator and her heart rate spikes like Pikes Peak and right, right—Colorado, she's in Colorado. Collbran. She's chasing—chasing the notebook, chasing the name, Mary Stitch, the woman Sugar's mother met here, the woman who can help her, can *cure her,* or at least show her the way out of this curse...

But that's all big-picture stuff. The little picture is: what?

Where is she?

What the hell happened to her head?

What hasn't happened to your head? a cruel little voice reminds. *Your head's been knocked around so much, it's like a battered wife. How many concussions is too many, Miriam? At what point does your brittle head crack like an egg and spill everything out—Humpty Dumpty won't go back together again.*

A tentative step forward. A small table. A lamp.

She reaches. Fumbles for a lamp chain. *Cuh-click.*

Light.

An attic. Unfinished. No drywall—blown-in insulation, exposed wood. Cobwebs. A big shape under a cover: a pool table, maybe. And some of it starts to come back to her: right, right, right, a modular house, two-story, set back on a property not far from the center of town, stuck way off one of those numbered nowhere roads here—58 and some fraction of a Road or something.

Then she sees it hanging by the door.

Every part of her goes cold. Her mind rushes backward through time, through memory, back under the river, in the gray churn of the rising waters—a young girl clutched in the hands of an old woman, bodies down there in the sweeping dark.

The river is rising...

Here, in this room right now, a living memory. Too real. Impossibly so. Hanging by the door, on a hook: a ratty brown cloak.

Attached to it, a mask. A hood. One she knows all too well. A long metal beak with nose holes punched out of it. Eyes are dead black goggles bolted into the leather. She can almost smell the funeral flowers burning. Can *hear* the man singing from inside the mask—*"May this a warning be to those / that love the ways that Polly chose / turn from your sins, lest you despair / the Devil take you without care."* "Wicked Polly," trilled by Carl Keener. The Mockingbird Killer—or one of them. Him and the whole Caldecott clan.

And there is his mask.

Downstairs: a man screams.

Then it's swiftly silenced.

Miriam feels in her pocket for her knife. It's not there. *I have another one. I'm sure of it. Somewhere...*

Footsteps coming closer.

It is what it is, Miriam thinks. And her hands curl into hard fists.

2

One Week Ago: The Bar Bet

The moon shines, captured in the waters of the Vega reservoir. Miriam sits at the bar, staring out the window at it, lost in the black waters, the white ribbons of light, the bands of clouds sliding over it all. She pops a chicken wing in her mouth—one of those funky ones with the two bones instead of one, where you have to navigate the gristle in your mouth—and vacuums the meat off it. The wing sauce is habanero hot, and it lights her up like a sacrificial pyre. After that, a sip of the margarita in front of her and a quick towel-off with a wet-nap before she takes a look down at the calculator watch on her wrist.

8 PM.

Late, late, late.

Of course.

You'd think a psychic would be on time.

There she sits. Idly kicking her boot-toe into the side of the bar. Behind her, the lodge is quiet—tables of dark wood, empty of guests. Still early in the season. Even though it's spring, there's still snow on top of some of the mountains, and up here, the chill in the air is something that crawls into you like worms using your skin for a blanket. A far cry from Florida.

Florida. Jesus. Ashley Gaynes. Her mother. Not to mention the thing with Louis. That phone call...

Fuck. Shit. *Shit fuck.*

Grief sucks at her like a leech.

It's good to be far away from all that. Because now she has a chance. A chance to change not just the fates of other people, but this time? Her own.

Movement next to her. Barstool groans against the floor as a man sits. He's got a face like a hatchet—all sides of it leading to a sharp, pointy front: chin, nose, the silver peak of his close-cropped hair. Even his beard is shorn high and tight, so clean and crisp, it looks like it could cut paper if you slid a piece along it.

The bartender—a woman built like a plow ox—comes up, says, "Whaddya say, John?"

"Janice," he says. Voice gurgly and growly. Once a smoker, maybe. Or just a guy who lived a rough life and gargled rocks. "Same old."

"Whaddya drinking?"

He gives her a grumpy, incredulous look. She laughs, and then pours him a beer off the tap. Dos Equis. He sips a bit of foam off the top, licks it from his lips, then says, "Hey, get me an elk chili, will you?" She nods and he calls after her, "Unless you got a prime rib back there for me."

She barks over her shoulder, "Keep dreaming, John."

Then she's gone through the kitchen doors.

He snorts: a hollow, maybe mirthless laugh kept to himself, for himself.

Miriam feels his eyes drift to her.

"You like prime rib?"

"Is this a dick joke? A come-on line?"

He's taken aback. His head lifts as his neck goes straight. "What?"

"I say, *Yes, I like prime rib.* And then you grab your salt-and-pepper yambag and give it a little jostle before saying, *Well, little lady, I got some prime rib right here.* And then we laugh and laugh and you think I'm going to go home and give your old dong a young-girl go, and what's really going to happen is I'm going to take my hot-sauce hands and smear them into your eyes, and then while you're there crying, I'm going to kick the stool out from under you. You'll fall like a sack of potatoes, maybe crack your head. And I'm going to walk out and the bartender's going to laugh at you as you piss yourself. The end."

"That's quite a story."

"I like to think of myself as a storyteller."

He sips the beer. "For the record, I was legitimately asking you about prime rib. Actual prime rib. They do it here Friday and Saturday nights. Tonight's Monday, though, so."

She takes a drink from her margarita. Licks a little salt off, lets it crunch between her teeth. "Oh, then yeah, I like prime rib. The bloodier, the better."

He holds up his beer. She takes hers and clinks it. "Cheers," he says.

"Back atcha."

They sit there for a little while. He finally says, "I'm not that fuckin' old."

"Great."

He turns. Now he's invested. Maybe even his feelings are hurt a little bit. Miriam always thinks it's hilarious how men act so tough like they're all steel rebar and beef jerky. In reality, men are soufflés: they puff up big but shrink fast at the slightest bump, shudder, or temperature dip. (Or maybe, she thinks, they're like the balls that dangle between their legs: they shrivel fast when it gets too cold and sweat lots when it gets too hot.)

"How old do you think I am?"

She arches an eyebrow. "I'm not a carnival game."

"Spare a Methuselah such as myself a moment of your insight."

She sighs. Groans. "Ugh. God. Okay." She looks him up and down. "You've got some mileage on you. Deep lines like tire treads, maybe a little dust and grit pressed in there. You're the rubber that met the road, huh? Still. You look tired, but your eyes, they got sparks jumping between them."

"And?"

"And what?"

"My age, goddamnit."

"Oh. Right." She clucks her tongue. "Let's go with...sixty."

"Sixty. You think I'm sixty years old."

Miriam shrugs, noisily slurps her margarita. "Am I wrong?"

John pauses. Pops his lips a few times. Then he laughs big and loud. "You nailed that right to the wall. I turned sixty just last week. You have a talent."

"Must be psychic," she says, and again raises her glass— she taps the base of hers against the top of his sitting there still on the bar. "Anyway. Happy birthday. I hope you got all that you wished for. And a blowjob. Everyone deserves oral sex on their birthday." She narrows her eyes and points an accusing finger. "Not that I'm offering, mind you."

He waves her off. "I've been with younger women, and you know what? Not worth it."

"Bullshit. You mean you wouldn't go a couple rounds with me in the sack? Old man, I'd rock your world so hard, your pelvis would shatter and you'd *love* every second of it. I'd suck the Lipitor right out of you. Bang you so hard, you'd temporarily forget that you are on the downward slide of your life and that the deep, dark dirt nap awaits as the expiration date on your mortality tip-toes closer and closer and closer— the Reaper creeping ineluctably toward your bedside."

"That's dark."

"That's life."

"You got that right. Where you're wrong is: the vigors of youth are nothing compared to the rigors of experience." He shrugs. "Besides, us old shrivs are grateful anytime wants to play with our balls or coochies. Two old folks together is two old folks very thankful someone wants to rub bits with them."

"I'm eating," she says, making a face.

"And apparently, according to you, I'm dying."

"We're all dying, John. Life wouldn't be life if it weren't for death."

"Profound."

"Just a little drunk. This is my third margarita and they make 'em strong."

At that, the bartender comes back out with a steaming bowl. Mounded with red chili, dark meat, melting cheese.

Janice opens a cupped hand; a couple lime halves spill out onto a cocktail napkin. John thanks her, starts squeezing the lime juice over the chili. He starts scooping it onto a spoon and blows on it to cool it.

Miriam says, "You know, my...dinner date is late, and you're the right age and the mood is about right. I have this... bar bet I make with people, sometimes older guys like you, and I haven't done it in a while."

"Oh, yeah?"

"Yep. Wanna hear the bet?"

He pops the chili into his mouth, fans his mouth as steam comes out. Around the mouthful of food he says, "Lesh hear it."

"I bet I can tell you how and when you're gonna die."

He smacks his lips, licks chili off them. Dabs at his beard with a napkin. "That's morbid."

"I figure we were headed that way already, but if I read you wrong—"

"No. I'm curious. You seemed to have a knack for guessing how old I am; maybe you can take a crack at imagining how I'll die."

She smirks. "I won't be guessing. I'll be telling you the facts."

"Facts about something that hasn't happened yet?"

"That's right. I really am psychic. I'll know, for absolute sure, how you suck the pipe. I'm no fake plastic Christmas tree, big fella, not just some pair of silicone tits bouncing like Jell-O molds: I am motherfucking *bona fide*, John."

A moment there, where he gauges her. A scrutinizing stare like each eye is a laser pointer going over her every inch. Is she bogus? Is she crazy? (*No to the former, yes to the latter*, she thinks.) And then he wipes his hands off on the napkin and he says, "Let's do it."

"First, a dollar amount. Fifty?"

It's then that Janice, the bartender, butts in. "Go lower, honey. John here just got laid off." Though she says with a twinkle in her eye, "To his credit, he still manages to patronize this fine establishment every night."

John smiles. "Same time every night, as a matter of fact."

It must hit him hard—the talk of him being laid off. Miriam can see that. He's trying not to let it, but he looks like he just got clipped in the nuts with a kid's Wiffle ball bat and he's trying not to look like it really hurts. He gives a sheepish grin and offers a shrug.

"Twenty," Miriam says. "Betcha twenty bucks."

"Done," he says. "So, how's this—"

But he sees her gaze flit toward the door of the lodge.

Someone comes in. A woman. Wide, swaying hips like the ass-end of a flightless bird. Draped in a colorful purple coat, poofy fur lining tucked under her neck, tickling her plump cheeks. The woman looks around. Spies Miriam. Gives a small nod.

You're late, bitch, Miriam thinks, but instead, she just holds up an index finger as if to say, *You need to wait.*

John follows the exchange, sees who she's gesturing towards. "I should've figured you two might've flocked together."

"You know her?"

"In a town under a thousand, one weird arty psychic broad stands out." Now he's uncertain, though. Guarded. Reserved. "This some kinda con?"

"It's not a con. I don't actually know—uhh, I forget whatever her name is. She left a card on my car a couple days ago. Wanted to meet, so here we are."

"Uh-huh. You know what? I'm good."

"You're good. You don't wanna see how you die?"

"I feel like...something shady is happening here. Getting a weird vibe."

"John, you don't wanna take the bet, don't take the bet."

He frowns. "Wouldn't a con artist say that?"

"I don't know what a con artist would say, because I am not a con artist." *Ashley was. He conned you good, didn't he?* She shakes that off.

"I mean, hell, how the hell does this bet even work? This is all theoretical, unless you're gonna pull out a pistol and shoot me dead here and now—and really, after the couple weeks I've had, please, consider it."

She starts to slide off the stool. Her boots clomp on the wooden floor of the bar. "You're ruining my flow, here, John, but here's how it works: I give you a twenty-dollar bill right now—" She fishes into her pocket, slides a crinkly bill out and waves it in front of him.

"This is how all cons start," he says. "Textbook."

She hisses, "Shut it, John—*a lady is speaking*. So. You take the money. You put *my* money in your pocket along with *your* money. You keep them there, always and forever, until the day comes that I have predicted your demise. If you don't die that day? Then the money is yours. Go buy something nice for yourself: a cat, a steak dinner. A geriatric hooker, perhaps."

"And if I die on the day? Then what?"

"Then I'll be there. Waiting. And I will take the money from your pocket, and I will go on my way, twenty dollars richer." She neglects to mention, *That is to say, if my schedule works out, and if your corpse isn't obliterated by a Mack truck, and if I'm not getting into some kind of other trouble that day.*

He stares for a minute. Like he can't even believe what she just said. Finally, he says, "In my life, I've heard some really goofy shit—and in the Army, I took some strange bets. I once ate the legs off a camel spider. I don't recommend that, by the way. But that was me, in a certain place, in a certain time. This isn't that. You know the phrase *Nie mój cyrk, nie moje małpy*?"

"Did you just have a stroke?"

"A Polish fella—a soldier—taught me that in Iraq. It means *not my circus, not my monkeys*. This bet is not my circus. And you are not my monkey." He gives an awkward smile. "You have a nice night, miss."

"Miriam. My name is Miriam."

But to that, he says nothing else.

And anger runs through her. Scampering fast. It strikes her, then, how completely she wants this: to touch him, to see his death, to watch him in the throes of future death— whatever death awaits. She feels like a dog watching a man eat a hamburger: so close, so juicy, yet *not in her mouth*.

You're an addict, she thinks.

Fuck you, she thinks right back. *I'm trying to quit.*

Sounds like what an addict would say.

Goddamnit.

She shoves the anger unceremoniously away—like lemmings urged off a cliff, little bitey furballs tumbling into the dark. Miriam grabs the rest of her margarita, polishes it off, and snatches a celery stick off her plate.

"Whatever, John. Good luck with whatever circuses and monkeys happen to be yours." It comes out petulant, pissy, but hey, fuck it. She owes him nothing and she's surprisingly stung by his rejection.

Then she's off.

She hightails it toward the door, where the woman in the purple coat stands, pursing her lips as if in a pout.

Miriam lifts her chin in greeting. "Hey."

"Are you Miriam?"

"Could be, rabbit. Could be."

"I have a message for you. From the spirits."

That, the woman says unironically. And out loud, for anybody near to hear.

Miriam scowls. "I hope by 'spirits,' you mean 'liquor.'"

Purple Coat leans in, an almost-beatific smile lifting her round cheeks. Her green eyes flash. "No, Miss Black. The spirits of those gone have seen your arrival here and they asked that we meet. They said you want something, and they want me to be the conduit that brings you answers. They want to help you. Help you..." Here she tilts her head like she's hearing music playing in another room and she's trying to figure what song it is. "Help you *escape* something."

Miriam chews on the inside of her cheek.

That's interesting.

"Oookay," Miriam says. "I'm ready to...accept the message. Let's hear it."

"We must go elsewhere for that."

That's how all cons start, she thinks before throwing a glance toward John still sitting at the bar. His back is to her. Drinking his beer. Eating his chili.

Asshole.

"Can I at least get your name?"

"I am Madam Safira Starshine."

It takes Miriam every molecule of willpower she can conjure not to burst out laughing. What the hell is wrong with people?

Still. She's intrigued. The hook is set in the meat of her cheek. Besides, what else is going on? John doesn't want her voodoo. She's not getting anywhere with this whole 'Mary Stitch' situation. No Louis. No Gabby. No anybody.

And so?

"Fine," Miriam says finally. "Let's roll."

3

Now: Footsteps Fast Approaching

ootsteps. Coming closer to the door. Miriam hunkers down.

Then the footsteps stop.

A voice—a woman's voice—calls through the door. "Miriam? I know you're awake. I heard you moving around. I'm coming in."

One moment. Two moments. Three. Then a squeak of a floorboard, a turn of the knob—the door starts to open inward. Part of a hand grabs the side of the door, eases it open. A shoulder. A glimpse of long, dark hair—

Miriam growls, kicks at the door. The door closes on the girl's hand. A cry escapes her: a vulpine scream. Miriam thinks, *Gotcha, bitch,* but then the door flies back open as the woman barrels through it. A flash of dark hair, a glimpse of green eyes, and a shine of white teeth. Something is in the woman's hand—not an axe but a hatchet, a hatchet like in the vision, and in that interstitial space between seconds, pieces start to fall into place, and suddenly Miriam knows who was screaming downstairs—though she doesn't know why, or how, or what yet is actually going on. It's not the blade of the hatchet that comes for her but rather the flat of it; it cracks against the side of her face as the girl backhands her with it.

Miriam's left heel skids out and she crashes down hard on her shoulder.

The woman stands over her. Panting. It's then Miriam sees:

She looks like me.

Same outfit: white, tattered T-shirt. Jeans rent by time and picking fingers. Black boots, too—Miriam's are Docs and so are the woman's. Scuffed and scraped in almost the same ways, the same places.

The woman blows a jet of air, lifting a frond of hair from her eyes.

The hatchet hangs heavy in the woman's hand.

"Miriam," she says. "Please. Don't do this. *Please.* Wait."

From the floor, Miriam snarls, "Who the fuck *are* you?"

"I'm Melora. I'm your sister."

4

ONE WEEK AGO: WINGED RATS, HOLY CHEESE

The woman drives a beat-to-shit VW Golf. Diesel. The headlights cut shaky yellow beams up the mountain road. The car bounces and shudders like it has the DTs. Ahead in the road, a pair of shining eyes. Something trundles in front of the car. A rangy, mangy thing: a fat possum. They wait for it to pass.

"I thought it would take more to convince you to come," Madam Safira Starshine (and again, Miriam works every muscle in her body not to explode in laughter) says. "The spirits said you were quite...stubborn."

"Well," Miriam says, "I like to keep things interesting. You think I'm gonna jump left or run right, and instead, I urinate in all your houseplants. I'm just tricky like that, I guess." She clears her throat. "Can I smoke?"

"Of course."

Miriam taps out a cigarette. Lights it with a Bic, rolls down the window a crack to blow the smoke. Cold air, sharp like thumbtacks, sweeps in over her.

The woman pulls past a mailbox from which hangs some kind of dream catcher—and then into a small lot where a doublewide trailer awaits.

A sign out front:

Madam Safira: Psychic Divination.

Mm-hmm.

Miriam rolls her eyes so hard, she almost breaks her neck.

The woman gets out. Miriam sucks on the cigarette greedily, flings it into a nearby birdbath. *Tssssss.* The outside of the trailer is a fenced-in miscarriage of lawn decor: a pink flamingo, a cheap mold-and-plaster version of the statue of David, another of Venus, three birdbaths, a brown bear on its hind legs carved out of a log.

Inside, the trailer isn't any better. Pink and purple curtains. Puke green carpet. More dream catchers. A black velvet painting of Engelbert Humperdinck—not that Miriam knows who the fuck that is, but his name is right there at the bottom of the "art" in glittery script. Plus, the standard trappings of a psychic faker: the crystal ball, the phrenology head, the Ouija board.

Shovelfuls of minor-league horseshit.

Right then and there, Miriam knows what her evening consists of:

Shaming this dumb, dumb woman.

A little part of her mind tries to convince her that this is the noble thing to do. Here's a woman, pretending to be a psychic and scamming people out of their money. Some of these psychics are basically vampires—shit, they're not even good enough to be vampires. They're leeches. Mosquitos. *Little ticks.* They latch on with their lying mouthparts and drink deep as they can, long as they can, pumping their own foul, diseased effluence right back into you.

But a more persistent voice reminds her, *You're doing this because she's trying to do what you do.* Trying to steal her thunder. A pretender to this already-dubious throne. And fuck her for that. A petty, cruel desire, perhaps, to toy with this woman, but Miriam wants what she wants. Sure as fate and death and all the other demanding forces of nature in this world.

Whatever. She knows how this is going to go. Safira Starshits is going to reach for the crystal ball. Or try to read Miriam's palm. Or feel her cranium for the bumps and divots of unforetold futures.

But that's not what happens.

Instead, she holds up a finger, encouraging patience. She ducks down a small hallway, then returns with an object: a large bell-shaped something draped in black cloth.

(If Miriam had to guess: a birdcage.)

Then she scoots past to the kitchen—which is barely a kitchen, really, as Miriam knows the layout well, having lived in trailers now and again. The kitchen is just part of the larger room—though this one is half hidden behind a shelf of all her kitschy psychic bric-a-brac. The sucking sound of a fridge opening. Then closing.

Something moves under the black cloth. The sound of clicking. Fluttering.

A bird?

Safira returns then with a small wooden cutting board. On that board: a glob of bone-white cheese shot through with arteries of something dark. The smell hits Miriam as it passes, a moldy, heady darkness to it. Musky, off, pungent as the congealed sweat on a dead man's scrotum.

Miriam scowls.

The woman pulls the cloth off the other thing—

And, sure enough, it's a birdcage.

With a living bird contained within. A pigeon, by the look of it. Head strutting like it's listening to music no one else can hear. Stepping left, then right, then left again. It coos and chirrups.

"Are you cooking dinner?" Miriam asks.

But Safira just smiles and pulls out a small, hooked knife. Oh. *Oh.*

Miriam's been around. She has, to put it plainly, *seen some shit.* Safira reaches in and withdraws the pigeon from its cage—this is a bird that doesn't squirm, that seems passive and even complicit in its own momentary demise. The woman takes the knife and, with one quick pull, pops off its head like it was a beer bottle in need of a swift opening.

Miriam feels it. A twinge across her own throat. Like a tightness in the esophagus. The bird's black eyes caught her in those final moments, glassily regarding her—and she felt the chance to become one with the creature as it died, to be drawn into its life force snuffed out.

She's glad that didn't happen.

With the head off, there arrives no great spray of blood, no gout of fluids. Just a trickle of dark red over Safira's rough knuckles. (Raspberry jam from a ruptured donut.) The headless bird continues moving. Little feet grabbing for ground that isn't there. Wings shrugging as if to say, *Yeah, so, I guess I'm dead?*

A sound comes out of Miriam. Somewhere between a laugh and a gasp. A shocked guffaw. Her mouth hangs open and only droops farther as Safira then—with what looks to be a practiced hand—draws the hooked blade down the center of the bird. Unzipping it like a coin purse.

Its guts fall out. Onto the cheese.

They plop and spatter. Red—almost black—blood like lava down a mountain of cheese. Guts atop it like a pile of earthworms.

Safira forms a claw with her left hand. And promptly begins to smash the mess together. Like she's working a dough. Claw, mash, lift, mash, again and again—the stink of coppery blood mixing with the rank stench of funky, fucked-up cheese climbs into Miriam's nasal passages and clings there like a ghost that won't be exorcised. She stops breathing through her nose but the smell still hangs there. Sucking tight to the roof of her mouth, the back of her throat, the deep of her sinuses.

"What the fuck," Miriam says. Less a question, more an exclamation.

"This is how we speak to the spirits. Those on the other side of the veil no longer speak our language—the tongue of the living, the words of the quick. The veil distorts and contorts our communication. And so we must create bridges. Ways to translate their words to ours, and ours back to them."

"Mashing bird bowels into disgusting cheese? You'd think a phone call would suffice." Miriam holds the back of her hand against her nose. "What about sexting? No sexting the spirits, I guess?"

"*Look*," Safira says, that one word lifted on a tide of genuine awe. "The way the cheese forms fissures—the moisture lost, broken, and here the blood crawls through these unexpected channels. It tells us so much."

"Be sure to drink your Ovaltine?"

Safira ignores her. Instead, the woman says:

"You're searching for something."

Sigh. "Yes, we've established that."

"An escape. An *end* to something." Then her eyes light up. Her awe deepens. "You are like me. You are a seer."

I'm nothing like you, moonbat. But—? Maybe that's not true. This woman knows things. She's receiving information she shouldn't have—admittedly, not in a way Miriam has ever seen before, but she's met how many other bona fide psychics? A half a dozen? Not even? What's to say what's normal with numbers that small? It'd be like meeting six girls and thinking you know everything there is to know about what it is to be female.

Maybe this "Safira" is the real deal, even if her name isn't.

"Go on," Miriam says, narrowing her gaze.

"You have come here. Looking for a woman. Melissa. Melora. Mary. *Mary.* Ciseaux. Stitch. Scissors."

Holy shit.

She knows.

She fucking knows.

Miriam says, "Tell me. I need to know." *I need to be rid of this power. I need to cut it the hell out of me.* This she says despite knowing she still wants it, too. It's like trying to kick heroin: she knows it's bad for her, but hey, how about one more hit? For old times' sake?

Then: Safira's eyes roll back in her head. Showing just the whites, like tops of skulls. Her head rolls around on her neck, loose, unpinned, a low whine from the back of her throat. Two fingers thrust down into the mash of blood and cheese, scoop a glob of the white cream and dark gore, and then begin to furiously scribble numbers—nine of them. *239159184.* The odor swells like a tide as what looks like some kind of grotesque miscarriage is stirred—like ghosts bothered out of their graves. Finally, a smear of viscera beneath it: a crass, violent underline.

As if for emphasis.

"I don't get it," Miriam says. "It's just... It's just a number." Nine numbers. What's nine numbers? A phone number has ten. Could be a social security number, maybe. Safira's hand, the one with the fingers dripping, goes to her face—she goes suddenly pale, a green color like something spoiled.

Then she turns and retches. Gagging. Dry-heaving.

"Get it away," Safira says. Words spoken through strings of spit.

Miriam looks down at the cutting board. The red mess. The glob. The string of numbers off to the side. Then she lifts it, takes back to the kitchen. Nearby, she spies a couple of pens in a ceramic mug that looks like a ladybug—its wings cracked and chipped—and then she pulls a swatch of paper towel off its roll.

She scribbles the numbers across it.

239159184.

Then: back to Safira.

"You okay?" Miriam asks.

The woman offers a meager, wan smile. "Yes."

"You look like kicked shit."

That earns from Safira a dark, bitter stare as response. But then she nods. "Speaking with the spirits is…not always pleasant. Their world is different from ours. A world of decay and madness. Even crossing momentarily to the other side is… harrowing. I'm sorry you had to see that."

Miriam folds her arms, shoving the flats of her hands under her pits. She needs another cigarette. "So, what does it mean?"

"What?"

"The number. What does it mean?"

"They don't explain themselves. It's a message. They expect you to understand it."

Miriam sneers. "Well, I *don't* understand it. The spirits can suck a bucket of ectoplasm through a long straw if they think I'm picking up what they're laying down. I don't speak numbers. I don't speak math." She holds up the paper towel and shakes it in the air. "This? Is useless to me. It might as well be a booby doodle drawn by some bored, horny kid."

The woman dabs at the corners of her mouth with a long, purple handkerchief. "I'm sorry. That was the message. They have no more for you."

"Great. Thanks." Miriam plunges an angry hand into her pocket, pulls out a dollar bill. That one hand crumples it into a boulder, and then she flings it into the woman's lap. "Thanks for absolutely nothing."

"I wish this was more helpful to you."

"Me, too. Can we go now?"

"Yes. I can take you to where you're staying…"

Which is a dinky-fuck motel off 70, and it's too far a drive and Miriam's now burning with a hot, high-fuel concoction of inchoate rage and utter bewilderment (with a splash of total desperation for good measure), and instead, she decides that she'd rather go back and drink more. A lot more.

"Take me to the bar. The lodge. Whatever it's called."

"Vega. Yes. Of course."

5

Now: Sestra

'm Melora.

I'm your sister.

She looks familiar. Miriam can't place it. But there *is* something about her.

"I don't know you," Miriam seethes, the side of her face pounding. Her tongue drifts across the tops of her back teeth, gives a little push. The tooth wobbles in the gum.

The woman smiles—a big, broad, manic grin. "We're sisters. We share...so much. We both drowned... the river, always rising."

It all starts to come back to her now. Her memories like the pages of a book flitting past. The number. The land. Pigeon guts mashed into soft cheese.

John. The Caldecotts. The swallow tattoo.

The vision.

"The Mockingbird Killer," Miriam says. "You. Still one of you left out here after all, isn't there? One more of your sick fuck family."

Melora looks aghast. Something well beyond insult. *Injured*.

"Oh, Miriam," she says. "There's so much you don't understand."

Miriam kicks her in the crotch.

6

ONE WEEK AGO: THE BAR BET, TAKE TWO

Safira says one last quiet apology. Miriam offers nothing in return. She gets out, and then Safira rolls down the window and says, her breath showing in icy puffs as she speaks, "The number must mean something, Miriam. Take heed."

"Uh-huh," Miriam says. "Thanks for nothing."

The VW Golf gutters and grumbles away.

"The whackadoo tell you anything good?" asks a voice behind her.

Miriam, heart suddenly fluttering like the wings of a startled sparrow, wheels, her hand already moving to her pocket where she keeps her knife. A quick part of her thinks, *I need to get more knives. Because knives are cool.*

It's John. He's standing behind one of the wooden posts holding up the overhang here at the lodge. He's got a crooked, hand-rolled cigarette hanging out of his mouth. "So?"

"I want one of those," Miriam says.

"It's weed," he says.

"It's not fucking weed. I know what weed smells like. It smells like a skunk that someone set on fire. That is high-grade tobacky of the non-wacky variety. And like I said, I fucking want one."

He laughs. Pulls out a little Altoids tin, and starts fishing for a hand-rolled cigarette. "I never took much to marijuana."

"Me neither, Grandpa."

He hands her the cigarette. Lights it for her, sheltering the match flame from the wind. Paper crinkles as it burns. She inhales. Smooth, like velvet.

Her skin tingles. Her lungs pulse.

"No," she says, blowing a jet of smoke from the side of her mouth. "The whackadoo didn't tell me anything good. Just a number."

"A number, huh? Phone number?"

"No. Only nine digits. So? Maybe a social. I dunno."

He shrugs. "Sorry."

"Yeah. Well. Life goes on."

"About that."

"About what?"

"Life. And its opposite."

"You wanna know," she says, a smile spreading across her face. The warm embers of satisfaction stir into a straight-up campfire in her belly. "That's what this is. I see your face, John Q. Jerkenheimer or whatever your name is."

"John Lucas." He takes one last hit off his cigarette and then flings it into the parking lot—a pinwheel of orange sparks in the night. "And yes, I would very much like to know. Miriam. Go back in? Let an old hound buy you a drink?"

"I'm still not going to fuck you."

"I still don't want you to."

"Then we're good. Let's go drink and explore the fun-tastic wonderland of one's own encroaching mortality!" She takes a few more sucks off the cigarette—like velvet, this smoke—and then they head back inside to the bar. Sit down at a booth. Order a couple white whiskeys. Something that comes from a bottle that looks like a pig. Same bartender: Janice.

As she brings the two whiskeys, Janice says, "She's not gonna do you, John. You know that, don't you?" Then to Miriam: "You're not gonna do him."

"It's not the plan, no," Miriam says, then tips back the whiskey. It cuts a burning channel right down her center. Like a core of lava boring down through her heart. John just waves both of them off, and Janice gives one last wipe-down of the table before retreating. To John, Miriam says, "So. Why now?"

"Why now what?"

"The decision to see." Part of her just wants to get into it. Grab his hand. Take the Grim Reaper's bone coaster through John Lucas's inevitable end. But her curiosity goes deeper than just his demise.

He sips at the whiskey. Winces. "Whiskey's not my thing." He clears his throat. "Anyway. I, ahh. I've been Army for a long time. Career. Or I thought. I was married. Have a son. The ex hates me. My son, well. He's..." His voice trails off. Whatever he was going to say, he drowns with another taste of whiskey— this one a gulp, not a sip. "I think it's just time to see what's coming for me."

"You want to see if it's something you deserve."

"I don't follow."

"Some people want to know how they kick off because... they think they can avoid it. Or because they like the idea of rubbernecking at their own death. It's like a fantasy, because in their hearts, they don't really believe that what I say I can do I can *really* do. You, though. You're one of those other ones. The ones who want to know if the way they go out is earned. Like maybe you've been spending your whole life buying your death in increments. All your moments cashed in toward a very specific grave plot." She finishes her own drink and feels for a second like she could breathe fire. She *urp*s into her fist. "What did you do in the military, John?"

He sniffs. "They called it, ahh, HIC. *Human Intelligence Collector.*"

"That sounds like something out of a horror movie."

He stares off at a fixed point about a million miles away. "Yeah. Probably about right. Truth of the thing is, I tortured people for information."

"Jesus."

"And I wasn't even the real deal. We just warmed up the poor bastards for the CIA. They're the ones who came in and… well. We don't know what they did, not exactly. They didn't want us in the room and they didn't record it, but, you know. You hear things. Half true, half something else, maybe. But even half true—even *one-tenth* of truth—that still gives me the piss shivers."

Miriam lays her hand out on the bar table.

She turns the palm up.

"Well, John, let's do this."

He looks down at it. Suddenly scared. She thinks, *Don't puss out on me now, dude. Give me my taste.*

John draws a deep breath.

Then he reaches down and plants his hand in hers—

7

One Week Ago: Wicked Johnny

ohn Lucas has been tortured.

His palms cut into Xs.

His head wreathed in a crown of barbed wire.

Something painted on his chest in blood—blood now dried, blood brown like rust and earth, blood that must be his. Blood that forms a bird with wide wings and forked tail: a swallow.

A shape roams into view. A tall figure with a leather hood. A hood that dead-ends in an all-too-familiar guise: a plague doctor mask. Long bird beak with holes cut in it. No smoke drifts, though, no smell of burned roses or crisped carnation, no funeral-flower incense—just the shiny glass eyes, the beak, the hood.

The figure holds a hatchet. Brand-new. Like for camping. It's all black. Matte. No shine. Just dull metal, swallowing the light.

"I'm glad I get to show you this," says a voice from inside the hood. A woman's voice. But someone else is there, too. Someone who stands behind it all, in the shadows, shifting from foot to foot. The hooded figure seems to be talking to this third person when she says: "You need to see this. You need to see what I've become."

Then the hatchet rises.

Then the hatchet falls.

But it isn't a clean strike. It's clumsy. Awkward. It doesn't take the head off, not like a heavy axe would—and so the Mockingbird lifts it and drops it again and again, chopping at John Lucas's neck like it's a stubborn branch or a bone in meat on the butcher's block. Chop, chop. He screams. Thrashes. Until his screams are drowned. Bubbling, gurgling. Chop, chop. Soon, the head rolls off the table. Still attached by a strip of long, lean skin.

One last hack. Cleaving that skin strip.

The head hits the floor with a thunk.

This happens in one week.

8

ONE WEEK AGO: FUCK THIS NOISE

And the vision kicks her in the teeth.

She yanks her hand away.

"Shit," she says.

He laughs a little like this is some kinda joke. "You okay? What'd you see? It's nasty, isn't it? Do I die on the toilet? My old man died on the toilet and—on the one hand, that's probably a good place to go in case you let everything loose when you go, but dignified, it is not—"

She can barely hear him.

The Mockingbird Killer. Alive? Is that even possible? Of course it is. Because it wasn't one killer. Carl Keener wasn't just one branch: their legacy grew in the twisted roots and black branches of a whole family tree. Beck Daniels. Eleanor and Edwin Caldecott. Who knows where else those tendrils grew?

"I have to go," she says.

"Wait—" He reaches for her. But his hand knocks over the whiskey—the glass rolls toward the edge of the table.

By the time it falls and shatters, Miriam is already halfway to the door.

9

Now: Mockery

The woman, Melora, doubles over—because while it isn't the same as a guy getting kicked in the soft, pliable sack that dangles between his legs, kicking a woman square in her lady-purse is no delight. Pain is pain, and this kind of pain is special—already the crazy bitch is clutching her middle as the feeling radiates up into her gut. She coughs. Winces.

On a resume, one of Miriam's talents would be *seizes opportunities*. Which she does now, launching herself up like a starving housecat. Claws out. Teeth bared. She slams into Melora. Her arms around the psycho's hips, head slamming right into the woman's middle.

The two of them topple.

Miriam pistons a fist—Melora turns her head, takes it on the cheek—

A roar of river water, a flurry of bubbles, rushing, gurgling. Like being smothered by it. In her ears. Up her nose. Overwhelming. Pulling Miriam down—

No vision. Just noise. *Melora is psychic.*

Real deal psychic.

Sister.

Oh, god.

Miriam's distracted, and Melora takes her shot—she flings her own elbow up, catching Miriam in the same place where the hatchet hit her moments ago. The ringing of a gong: everything vibrating, banging, cymbals going off in her head like someone sat an orangutan at a drum kit.

"We're... not supposed to be fighting," Melora stammers. She sounds sad, desperate, panicked. "We're sis—"

Miriam pins her with her knees and then backhands her. *Whap.*

"We're not fucking sisters," Miriam hisses. "I don't *have* a sister."

"No, not like that," Melora says, the fight gone out of her. Her hands fall flat to her sides, thudding against the floor. "You fell into a river. Down there, in the dark. I was there, too. I was drowning, too."

Miriam almost laughs. "Jesus Christ on a Creamsicle. You really are nuts." She remembers being down there in the dark of the river. The shadows moving. The water rushing. All the world sounding like blood rushing in a giant's ear. Eleanor Caldecott there in the deep. Holding Lauren Martin—*Wren.* Other bodies down there, too. Ghosts. Visions. Not real. Right?

Beneath her, the woman makes a low, keening, grief-struck sound. "I'm so sorry, Miriam. I'm so, so sorry."

For a half second, Miriam is like, *Sorry for what?* She's about to ask, about to say, *This is what you wanted. This is who you are, some crazy Caldecott remnant who thinks she can hang with...*whoever the others were to her. Cousins, uncles, distant relations, lost brothers, blah blah blah.

But then—a sharp stick in the top of her thigh, just south of her ass cheek.

A needle prick.

Her gaze darts. She sees Melora's hand there. Holding a small, disposable injector. She tries to read what's on the side. Can't. Vision already going smeary.

If I'm going dark, you're coming with me, she thinks, and reaches down to wrap her hands around Melora's neck. The psycho's eyes bulge. Tongue out. But then it's like Miriam's hands go soft. Disconnected. Like gloves that someone staple-gunned to the end of a pair of pool noodles. Can't get a grip.

Everything starts to go slack.

Melora gives her a gentle urging. Protects her landing.

She doesn't go out. She doesn't fall unconscious. Her eyes stay open. Everything feels like it's floating. The floor disappearing beneath her. The ceiling and roof drifting up into the star-scattered sky. Her breathing goes slow. Shallow.

Melora stoops down. A small, soft smile. "It was the only way," she says.

10

SIX DAYS AGO: TRESPASSERS

ornings, Miriam thinks, can go eat a dick. They can go eat a dick salad with a few extra squirts of smeg-sauce. Topped with cock-waffles. Further topped with jizz syrup. All served in a roasty-toasty bowl of crispy, deep-fried dog shit. Mornings can eat all that, then jump off a cliff and into the mouth of an alligator. An alligator with a righteous case of irritable, inflamed, prolapsed bowels.

Fuck mornings.

For real.

Mornings mean the night is over. Mornings mean sleep is done, game over, goodbye. Mornings are the consequence of your actions, the culmination of the twenty-four–hour equation. They're like being born all over again. Emerging into a bright, nasty, stupid world. Mouth tasting of ash. Eyes seal-coated with sleep-boogers. Hair looking like you just went ten rounds with the Devil his own self.

The curtains to the rinky-dink motel room—a room that smells of must, and dust, and mold, all of it with a strange minerally tang like she's down in the bowels of a silver mine somewhere—whip open suddenly.

They do this by someone's hand other than her own.

A dark shape stands by them.

Which means, *Oh, god, did I fuck somebody last night?*

It happens. It happened with Gabby. Drinking plus visions often means...

The dark shape steps forward, at first framed by the light—just a tall, broad-shouldered shadow. But it's a shape she knows. One cut from big cloth.

Louis.

"Wake up, muffin," he says, singsongy.

His voice is rich, loamy. Wet, too. Like he's speaking through a mouthful of moist cake and earthworms. His laugh is rocks in a cup. His breath is wind through dead trees.

"Fuck you," she tells the Trespasser. "Close the curtains."

"What are we doing here, Miriam?" he asks, sitting down. It's been a while since she's seen him. Now he's in the light. She sees the black Xs of electrical tape crossing his one eye. Sees the scabby knuckles and the cracked lips. She blinks, and then he's different: the young black boy from Philly. One untied shoelace. A gun in his hand, shaking with ego and fear. Blink again and now it's Gabby with her cut-up face, blink again and it's Miriam's mother sitting there in the chair with empty eyes and a mouth frozen in an eternal howl.

One last blink and it's back to Louis.

Or Not-Louis.

"You know what I'm doing," she groans, and hides under the pillow.

Suddenly, he's there. Standing over here. He whips the pillow off her head. The light's bright—too bright. She smells his breath: the smell of rank river water, the stink of fish washed up on a muddy bank. "You can't get rid of me," he says.

"I can. And I will. I'm getting close. I can feel it."

"Is this what you really want? To be shut out from your power?"

She squeezes her eyes closed. Hard. "It's not *power*. It's a *curse*. Somewhere out here is the start of a thread. A thread named Mary Stitch. I'm going to pull on that thread and I'm going to follow it. At the end of it, I'll have a way out. An exit from all this—" And here she thinks but does not say, *An exit that doesn't include me putting a gun in my mouth or opening my wrists in a hot tub.* "Now fuck off in some other direction and let me sleep."

"You *are* sleeping," he says. "And it is a power. I could've died. I *would* have died—up there in that lighthouse, a fillet knife in my brain."

"Maybe you wouldn't have been in that lighthouse if I hadn't climbed into your rig in the first fucking place. Oh, and you're not *you*. You're not him."

"Yes. That's right. Louis isn't here with you, is he?"

The way the Trespasser says it, petulant, mocking, some real *nanny nanny boo boo* bullshit. It ticks her off. She snarls. Launches herself out of bed, claws out, raking them across his face—

Skin peels away. Underneath: mealworms squirming, pill bugs tumbling.

He laughs, reaches for her, gives her a hard pull—

Wham. She slams against the carpet.

A hard, sucking gasp.

The room is dark. The curtains closed.

The phone is ringing.

Not her cell. The motel phone.

She grunts. Stays on the floor and paws upward, hand feeling along the bedside table. Thump, thump, scrabble—ahh, the phone. Off its cradle, into her hand, against her ear.

"Wuzza," she mumbles.

"It's me," says a voice. A voice that clarifies: "It's John. I guess we don't know each other enough to get away with *it's me*."

"Muzza."

"You wanna get some breakfast?"

"Bruhfuss. Yah."

He's still talking, but she plops the phone back on the cradle. That one word—*breakfast*—is enough to wake her up. Because mornings may suck, but they are redeemed by the power of motherfucking breakfast foods.

11

SIX DAYS AGO: BRUHFUSS, YAH

Breakfast joints—cafes, coffee shops, diners—are her thing.

But this is the first time she has dined in a bait shop.

Because that's what it is. A bait shop. Rods and reels hanging from hooks emerging out of wood paneling. An old, dusty, wood floor. An actual refrigerator case of bait just three feet to her left: earthworms, minnows, little cups of chum.

When they enter, she makes a joke: "You know I'm not a largemouth bass, right?" And John laughs a little, and then she says, "You're supposed to make a joke back at me like, 'You're no bass, but you sure got a large mouth.' Or maybe 'With as big a mouth as you have, I got confused.'" And he just looks at her like she's got a dick for a nose, and then they sit because, as it turns out, this bait shop also serves breakfast. One kind of breakfast: breakfast sandwiches.

Which are some of Miriam's favorite things.

Because breakfast is amazing.

And sandwiches are amazing.

And when the two of those things have a warm, cheesy, carb-swaddled baby? Well. It's probably why mankind evolved at all.

So there they sit, near the bait case. Eating sandwiches.

"You guys don't have pork roll out here," she says, cheek bulging with food. The words come out more like *You guysh don haf pork roll out here.*

John shakes his head. "No, I don't think we do."

"Scrapple, either."

"We do have elk burgers. And great tacos. And Rocky mountain oysters."

"Those are testicles."

He shrugs. "Bull balls. Yep."

"You're gross. You're lucky I got a stomach like a cast-iron cook pot."

He's staring out over a bagel sandwich. Not eating it. "You still owe me."

"Hunh?" She swallows a cheesy, meaty, eggy clot. "Oh. Your death."

"That's right."

"I, ahh. I haven't figured out what I want to do about that yet."

He arches a fuzzy, gray eyebrow. "I don't follow."

You die in a week, John, she thinks. *And you die by a hand that is somewhat familiar to me. And I don't want any part of it. I want to eat this sandwich and I want to run away. I want to leave you to your doom.*

Cold. Horrible. Makes her feel bad for thinking it; and Miriam, she's not super-used to feeling guilty or shameful. But this is that. John dies on that table, beheaded by some amateur-hour Mockingbird Killer and... c'mon.

But still? *This isn't why she's here.* She's here to get rid of this power. Not get tangled up in someone else's net. Her getting involved is complicated. Maybe it's time to just let one slide. Let the rope slip her grip.

The voice of the Trespasser whispers:

You thought you killed the Mockingbird, didn't you?

Doesn't that make this a little bit your fault?

"I'll cut you a new deal," John says, cutting off her awkward, thinky silence. "Maybe I help you in a way and you still tell me about my death."

"Help me? How?"

"That number."

"The number from Madam Safira Scooby Snacks?"

"Safira's her real name, though obviously Starshine isn't, but yeah. That's the number I'm talking about."

She leans forward, chin in her tented hands. Gaze suspiciously narrowed.

"Go on," Miriam says.

"It's nine digits. I worked for a little while at GVP—Grand Valley Power. Meter reader. And out here—hell, maybe in a lot of places—we would go by this thing called the APN: assessor's parcel number. We didn't worry about addresses because the APNs were more accurate and meaningful. Out here? Those digits are nine numbers. I thought maybe..."

"Hm. Shit. Maybe."

"Gimme the number," he says. "I'll run it through a real estate friend."

"And then?"

"I get you what you want, you tell me about my death."

"I'm in. But be honest: you don't even really believe I have the power. I can see it in your eyes. You think I'm selling you a case of snake oil."

He chuckles. "Not exactly. I think *you* believe it."

"So, why? Why even ask."

"Honestly? I'm bored, for one. Two, I'm used to getting what I want. I don't mean that in a childish, petty way, though that's probably part of it and probably part of why my wife left me and my son..." Here his face twists up like a wrung mop. "Why my son is such a *fuck-up*." Way he emphasizes that must mean the kid is a real mess. "I haven't seen my boy in forever and he's just on the other side of the state—I'm getting off track here. What I'm saying is, you're dangling something in front of my face. And I want it. That's what they teach us as interrogators. To go and get, at any cost."

"So, this is the carrot."

"Mm-hmm."

"But we haven't seen the stick."

He grins. "I'm too old to give you the stick, sweetheart." But she's not sure. There's a glimmer of something dark there. Like the shine off black hematite. "You want me to call my friend?"

One last bite of sandwich popped in her mouth. Chew, chew, chew. She nods as her jaw works the sandwich. "Do it, dude. Do it up."

On the way out, she heads to the counter to pay—her treat, she says.

She looks at the extra bits for sale on the counter. Tic-Tacs and keychains and fisherman bric-a-brac. And little knives, too. Huh.

12

Now: K-Hole

We all float down here. A line from a book. A book about a clown that wasn't a clown. Staring out from under the street, underneath a sewer drain. A giant spider. A preteen orgy. *It.* One of the books that Miriam kept hidden from her mother: that, *The Shining*, a book called *Swan Song*, another one called *Lost Souls*. A Ramones album. A stack of *Batman* comics. Little secrets kept under floorboards in her closet, some kept hidden in a stump out back of the house. *They'll corrupt you*, Mother said. *All you need is this.* She handed Miriam a Bible as she burned the books, the CDs, the comics—the smell of paper crisping, the smell of plastic melting. The taste of tears and snot. Precious gifts of sounds and story carried away by tongues of flame, and here she thinks, *Why am I thinking about this?* and then, *Oh, right, because I feel like I'm floating.*

Her head thumps against each step. Brought downstairs on a comforter dragged by a woman named Melora. Miriam can't feel the stairs hitting her at the back of her neck, the base of her skull—like riding marshmallows, like pillows and clouds and other soft things. The woman speaks as she drags Miriam:

"You drowned and I drowned and that's when we became one. That's when the door opened and I could see things. I could see through your eyes. I could see the stains of sin on people."

Miriam tries to speak, but what comes out is a mushy gabble.

"We have to kill him," Melora says. "I want your blessing. I need it. He's a bad man. Everyone knows you've been seen with him, but this is my chance to do right. To fix broken things. John Lucas is a killer. And a rapist. I have proof. He would've done you, too. But I'm saving you. I'm saving us both."

You bitch, you stuck me with a needle. She tries to say that but, again, it's just her mouth working and nonsense sounds coming out. Like she had a stroke and her mouth isn't connected to her brain. Nothing is. All her limbs have the puppet strings cut. She tries to move. They twitch. Not much else.

Thump, thump, thump.

Bottom of the steps.

Louis, Not-Louis, now hovering above her. In the air like a ghost—arms gone to vapor at the ends, blood-slick hair drifting and splaying like seaweed swaying. His mouth moves but the words don't speak out loud so much as they appear inside her mind, echoing: *You tried to run away from us, Miriam, but you ran right toward us. Funny how you do that. You think you can avoid going left by going right, but you always come back around, don't you?*

She tries to say, *I have a choice. I am the one with all the choice. I'm the riverbreaker, I'm fate's foe, I'm—*

But Louis just laughs inside her mind.

Then, Melora returns. Didn't know she was gone but now here she is again, tugging on a hood over her head. A leather hood with a metal beak. Eyes barely seen behind the shine of glass goggles.

"I had this made special," she says. "Do you like it?"

13

Four Days Ago: Buzzard Creek

The day is warm. The sun is bright and bold, like a fist on the back of Miriam's neck. She stands on the side of a road, a road without a name, a road with just a number because as John put it, *That's just what they do here.* Here, on 58 6/10 Road, she looks out at an open property. No house. No driveway. Just a mess of trees—white aspen amongst some scrubby pines—on a bulging berm. In the middle of it, an ill-seen, bubbling creek.

John says, "This is it. This is APN 239159184. That's Buzzard Creek cutting its way through the ground out there. Running hard right now with all the snowmelt coming down."

"It's nothing. There's nothing here."

"That's mostly true. It is pretty, though."

"I don't give a monkey's balls about pretty. This wasn't it, then. Your theory didn't work." Her hope is a bird shot out of the sky: *kablam.*

John shrugs. Sighs. "Sorry." He flips through some pages in his hands, pages sitting in a manila folder. "You sure your psychic friend is the real deal?"

"I'm not. I don't even know that she's really a psychic."

"She didn't used to be. Used to be an actress in Denver."

An actress? Doesn't that figure. All those theatrics. Still, though—that was more than what she expected when it came to *commitment to the role.* Killing a pigeon and smashing its guts into a glob of cheese? And she *knew* things. Things that almost no one is privy to. She knew Miriam. Or part of her, at least. "Worthless woman," Miriam says. "Nothing here. And no one."

"You wanna know who owns it?"

"Huh?"

He taps the folder. "The property. Someone bought it."

She reaches out an open palm, waggles her fingers.

He puts the papers in her hand.

When she pulls them close, she sees it. The name.

"Oh, shit," she says.

The owner of the property?

E. Caldecott.

Fuck.

14

Now: The Stalking Horse

Melora turns the hatchet in her hand. "I'm not a Caldecott. You know that by now, don't you?" She *hms*. "Maybe you don't. I just needed to get you here. I thought it was... I dunno. Appropriate? At the time you were in the river with Eleanor Caldecott, I was in the bathroom with my boyfriend. He'd beaten me pretty good. My eye was swollen up. Had a good knot on my head. Kyle—that was his name, Kyle—he dragged my butt into the bathroom and conked me on the toilet tank, then tried to drown me in the tub. And I guess he did. Paramedics said I died. I was down there in the water like that, his hand holding a clump of my hair, my blood swimming out in front of me, turning the water red, and I saw someone. I saw you. I saw you reaching for a young girl. I saw a man coming up behind me. It was a heckuva thing, like I wasn't just there in the tub but like I was at the bottom of that river, staring up from the mud. We connected. And ever since, I've been able to feel you out there. Sometimes, I can see through your eyes, too. I know you. We're sisters. Sisters of the spirit. Of the soul. You can see that, right?"

Miriam's mind swims.

Nearby, she hears John grunting, groaning, weeping.

"Something else changed for me, too. I can see people who have done bad things. Really bad things. It leaves a…a mark on them. Like these striations of death. Like rigor mortis. When a dog dies, you can see them form first on its belly—these long, gray fingers, like stains on the skin. I'm a vet tech, by the way, and I dosed you with ketamine. That's why you can still see and hear me." She breathes loudly inside the mask. "I used xylazine to knock you out first." She laughs like this is funny, somehow. "I put that in a dart. Had it ready. When you started to come out of it—*then* the ketamine. I think it's working. It's working, right?" Another laugh. Some joke Miriam doesn't get.

Miriam tries to struggle. Her body is gone from her. Like it's somewhere else, like her mind is unmoored and hovering above it all.

She tries to speak, too. A sound comes out: "Whhha. Mmmmn. Puh. *No*."

"Your friend, John. He's a bad fella. He's done wrong. And we're gonna right those wrongs today—help get some justice for poor girls. See, I've been studying that Caldecott case. It hit the news, you know. Some Internet sites and forums even have glimpses of you—they think you're some kind of *avenging angel.* Maybe not even a real person but some kind of ghost. Anyway. The Mockingbird Killers, they killed girls. Hurt them. But now, I thought, I can use that. Like, what's the word? Subvert. I can *subvert* that. Turn it on its ear. Hurt the men who hurt women. Lay them on the table. Make those wicked fools pay."

Miriam feels hot tears creep down her cheek.

Behind Melora, Not-Louis stands, licking his lips. Then he's gone.

"Like my boyfriend. I'll get him someday, too. He ran. I'll find him. You'll help me find him. Because like I said, we're sisters. I love you. So, so much." She stoops down, kisses Miriam's forehead. The kiss is cold and soft. "Now, let's kill John Lucas. You saw the photos I left for you?"

15

ONE DAY AGO: GONE JOHN

While she's out trying to chase down leads on this Mary Stitch character, John leaves a message for her at the motel—literally, a note taped to her front door: *Come to my house. Got info. 4040 Durant Gulch.*

She takes the pickup truck—an old beat-ass thing she purchased from some gator wrestler in Florida—and heads out that way after a time to look at the road atlas in the glove compartment. Durant Gulch is a long, winding road that parallels a deep, red-rock ditch. Goes up, up, up, and close to the top, she finds his house: a little rancher. Humble. Not much to look at.

The door is open. Just a little.

She thinks, *I hope like hell he left it open for me*, because the alternative…

The door drifts all the way wide.

"John?"

Nothing. No one answers.

Shit, shit, shit.

There, on a little nook table with a simple red tablecloth: two manila folders like the ones he was holding. The first and closest is open. Miriam picks up papers, skims them. The E. Caldecott who owns parcel number 239159184 accepts mail at a different address. Just outside of Collbran, in a town called Fruita.

John said he'd have his real estate buddy do a little more digging. Was this the result of that? Sure looks like it.

But then, the other folder.

That one has a Post-it note on it.

Her name is written on that note. In a script different from the one left at her motel room, the one from John. This: red pen. Flowy handwriting.

All it says is:

Miriam.

Miriam opens it.

Her innards clench.

Pictures. Crime scene photos. Marked at the bottom with *Denver PD.*

Dead women. Girls. Teenagers, maybe. Six of them, at least. All beaten so that their faces are unrecognizable. Hair matted with so much blood.

Miriam doesn't understand what she's looking at.

Her breath comes in fast, shallow bursts. Heart racing. Throat burning with bile. She thinks, *This is tied to the Mockingbird Killers somehow,* and again she starts concocting a mad idea in her mind about a resurgent Caldecott clan out there killing young women. But she tries to imagine how John ties into it. He dies soon at the hands of one of them, but that doesn't track: they kill girls, like the girls in these photos— bad girls, Wicked Pollies—not old men from the Army. More theories: maybe John *is* one of the Caldecotts, maybe he's been playing her this whole time, and maybe that blows back on him somehow.

Maybe he killed these girls.

She turns over the photos. Writing on the back of each. A time and a date. Each written in the same handwriting on the note she found at her door.

John's handwriting.

Miriam slams that folder closed.

She picks up the other one. The one with the address on it.

Time to take a trip, she thinks.

But first, she has a few stops to make.

16

Now: Death Marks

Melora walks over to Miriam. Helps prop her up. Miriam's like a doll: *Pose me, place me, use me.* When it comes to date rape drugs, the one everyone always talks about is Rohypnol, or *roofies*. But ketamine is right up there, too.

Something rattles in Miriam's boot. Something loose.

Again, Melora kisses her on the cheek. "You stay there. Watch me. I'm just like you, Miriam. You're not alone anymore. I know you feel alone, but you have me. Someone to do what you do. To make the bad people pay."

Then it all starts to happen like in the vision.

Miriam realizes, *I'm the one standing there. In the back. Just a shadow.* The killer's not talking to somebody. The killer's talking to *her.*

I really am just a shadow. Bodiless, thin, bleak, black.

Melora goes to John. John, who cries and struggles and bleeds.

Hatchet in Melora's hand.

Do something, Miriam screams inside her own mind. *Move. Speak. Something. Anything!*

Melora says, "I'm glad I get to show you this. You need to see this. You need to see what I've become."

This is happening. You have to stop it.

Change fate.

Rock in the river time.

Melora lifts the hatchet.

"Wait," Miriam says—an animal bleat. She lifts her hand. Waves it about.

The killer stops. Hatchet hanging.

Melora turns toward her, the beak pointing, the leather hood creaking.

"We...do it..." Miriam draws a deep breath through her nose. "*Together.*"

"Together," Melora repeats, the word hollow inside the hood. A few seconds pass. Seconds that feel like minutes. Miriam still floats. Disconnected. The wall behind her barely a presence at all. But then Melora says, "Yeah. *Yes.* I like that. We should do it together. You can… you can show me the way."

She steps toward Miriam. *Sisters.* Arms out. Helping Miriam to move, one plodding step at a time. Toward John there on the table. His eyes big as dug graves. Fearful as he's probably ever been. Are these his sins coming home to roost? Does he believe he deserves this?

Whatever comes next, it has to happen a certain way.

My boot.

It's in my boot.

Miriam doesn't have much strength. She still feels off-kilter, unmoored, and so as they get to the table, she lets the weight of her body do the first part—she puts all her weight to her left side and falls that direction.

Into Melora. A moment of imbalance—

A moment of distraction.

Just enough for Miriam to grab the knife.

The second one.

The one she bought at the bait shop after breakfast that day. The one she bought just in case. A second knife—*because knives are cool.*

This one, hiding in her boot.

She grabs it—it's small. Three-inch blade. Serrated.

Opens with a quick flick.

A fast plunge and it sticks in Melora's thigh. The girl howls—and again the hatchet rises. Miriam, still sluggish, still groggy, can't do anything, can't be fast, so all she can do is *push* with all her might—

Melora falls.

The hatchet clatters.

Melora, on all fours, straining for the knife jabbed in her leg. Miriam has nothing, no grace, no dexterity, and even though control of her body is returning, the best she can do is drop down on her "sister" like a felled tree. One hand clumsily wrenching the hood up and off. The other arm snaking around the girl's neck. Miriam puts all her weight, meager as it is, straight down. Pulling her own arm tight. Grabbing her wrist with her other hand to cinch the noose.

Melora starts making a choking sound.

"I'm sorry," Miriam mutters. "I'm so sorry."

You can't live. You can't make these decisions. You can't be me.

I don't even want to be me anymore.

The woman's legs kick out.

Her head tries to snap back but there's nowhere to go.

And eventually, the fight goes out of her.

And death enters in.

17

Now: Time Keeps On Ticking

Rest. No rescue for John. No resurrection for Melora.

Miriam slumps against the wall and she sleeps. If it can be called that. Instead, it's like falling: falling down through the dark, through grave dirt, through a casket-shaped hole carved out of a hill. Rustle of feathers. Clack of beaks.

Eventually, she jars awake. To the sound of John Lucas weeping.

Her head feels like someone filled her sinuses with cement. Her body like someone injected molten lead into her bone marrow.

Somehow, though, she stands.

"You," she says. A frog croak.

John startles. Sniffs. His lip slick with snot. "Miriam."

"John."

"You killed her."

"I killed her."

"Thank you, thank you, thank you so much. Those girls, I, I, I didn't—"

Miriam sighs. "I know you didn't. The murders happened in Denver. At times you couldn't have done it. I stopped by the bar. Spoke to Janice. She confirmed for me that you haven't missed a night at the bar in... six months, maybe more. Two of those dead girls were in the last three. Wasn't you."

"Good. Good. Please...help me up."

She sniffs, clucks her tongue. "Not yet, Big John. Just because you didn't kill those girls doesn't mean you weren't responsible."

"What? I...Wait. Wait."

But she keeps talking. "You had those photos at your house. And that was your handwriting on the back. Janice told me something else, too, when I went by the bar." Miriam leans forward, trying not to fall over. "I asked her about your family. She said your son, David, lives out in Denver."

"Oh, Jesus. I'm sorry. I'm so sorry."

"You sired a killer. Your son killed those girls."

By now, he's sputtering. Mouth strung with bloody spit. "I wasn't sure. I had a friend on the force out there. Old Army buddy. He... he got me those photos. But... yes. Yes. It's him. I think it's him." He weeps. "I fucked up. I was a bad father.

Never there. My wife…my son. Oh, jeez, god. I didn't…" His words break apart like rotten bark off an old tree. He just makes a sad, angry sound.

"You did fuck up, yeah."

"Are you going to kill me?"

"I want to make a new deal with you, John. This one's not a bet. You won the bet we made already because as it turns out, you're not going to die like I said. You survived that because of me, and now your fate is again your own. But I own you. I own you right now because I could still cut your head off."

"Anything. Anything. Whatever it is, anything."

"You need to take care of your boy."

"Wh… what?"

"You need to go to him. And you need to stop him. I would. But I have other things to accomplish. I tire of all this. I want out. But you? You're just getting in. You promise me you'll stop your son."

"I promise."

"Do what's right, John. This *is* your circus. He *is* your monkey."

"I will. I will."

"Good."

And with that, she begins to undo his bonds.

18

Now: Stitches & Starshine

Safira enters her home. First thing she does, as many do: She flips on the lights.

"Hey," Miriam says. The little knife in her hand. Flipping around the way a magician moves a quarter around his knuckles.

"You."

"Indeed. I am me. A profound statement if ever there was one. *I am me.* A big, badass, ego-fed statement. I am me, and nothing will change me. It's sick because, honestly? I feel really empowered by that. And yet, at the same time, hamstrung by it, too. Because I don't want to be me anymore. I don't want what I have. Thing is, I wanted that so bad that I got roped into your lies. I should be smarter than this. *Faster.* And yet you snookered me, Starshine."

"Miriam, it wasn't me."

"I know. It was your sister." Fear dashes across Safira's face. "You're wondering how I know. It's not just that you guys looked alike. It's that, in her wallet, she kept a crumpled-up picture of you. Sweet, I guess, at least until you realize she wanted to be *my* sister more than she wanted to be yours."

"I... I'm not a real psychic."

"No shit, Shoeshine. That's why you puked, isn't it? You put on too much of a show and... you were in too deep. The blood. The cheese stink. Too gross for you by a country mile, so next thing you know: *blargh.* Yak chowder."

Safira's silence answers that question.

"My sister, Melora, she said it had to look good. Melora—"

"Is dead."

That, she didn't know. The stunned look on her face shows it.

"...why?" That question spoken with a trembling tongue. Trying not to cry, maybe. Trying to keep it together.

"Because she was going to kill the wrong guy. She was about to make an epic mistake. And because she was fucked up. Broken. When she died the first time, it cracked that mirror good. And you can't put a mirror back together again, Safira. There will always be those faint lines, those shatter marks. And because ultimately, I don't like someone being in my head. Seeing through my eyes. I don't know how she did it and I don't care. I didn't want to kill her. I wanted to help her. But fate, you see—fate is feisty. I let her go, that death she desired—the death she *committed* to with her actions—would still happen. Fate's a rubber band that way—you can stretch it wider, wider, wider, and as long as it doesn't break, it'll always snap back into the same goddamn shape. So, you need to snip the rubber band. The only way to freedom is to *cut those bonds.*"

"Please… I didn't mean for any of this to happen. Not like this."

She's scared.

Good.

"I know you didn't, Sunshine. But what happened, happened. And now your cuckoo sister is dead—your fault for putting this all in motion."

"She wouldn't be denied—"

"I denied her. And now I'm about to hurt you, too, for making me do that. For throwing this noose around *my* neck. I'm trying to be good. Trying to be *better*. And you and your bugshit crazy sister drag me back into it. But I'm going to give you a chance to wriggle out. To go on your merry way— well, probably not so merry, because you'll always have that albatross around your neck, won't you? That dead bird with Melora's face."

"Anything. *Anything.*"

"I want to know where Mary Stitch is. You probably don't know. And if you don't? So be it. But there will be consequences to your unlucky ignorance, Safira. Real, bloody consequences. So, know anything? Will you get lucky? Let's spin that roulette wheel, see where the little ball lands."

Safira's words are breathy and buoyant with fear—

But also ragged with relief.

"I know about her. I do! I do. Not a bluff. She's... she's gone, long gone, gone for many years. But her brother, her older brother is here. Weldon. He's an old man now. No friends, not in the phone book, and the only reason I know anything about him is that I used to clean the cabins he rents—he rents them through a company, not directly, but I did the housecleaning when I was a girl."

"He's still alive?"

"He is."

"And you can give me his address?"

"I can."

"Good. Get a pen and write it down. Because I'm in a hurry."

In a hurry to find Mary Stitch.

And end this curse.

ABOUT THE AUTHORS

DELILAH S. DAWSON is the *New York Times* bestselling author of *Star Wars: Phasma*, as well as *The Violence, Bloom*, the Blud series, the Shadow series (written as Lila Bowen), and over two dozen more books and comics for all ages.

KEVIN HEARNE is the *New York Times* bestselling author of the Iron Druid Chronicles, the Ink & Sigil series, the Seven Kennings trilogy, and co-author of the Tales of Pell with Delilah S. Dawson.

CHUCK WENDIG is the *New York Times* bestselling author of *The Book of Accidents*, *Black River Orchard*, and the duology of *Wanderers/Wayward*, plus over two dozen other books for adults and young adults. A finalist for the Astounding Award and an alum of the Sundance Screenwriters Lab, he has also written comics, games, and for film and television. He is known for his popular blog, terribleminds, and books about writing such as *Damn Fine Story*. He lives in Bucks County, Pennsylvania, with his family.

9 781998 390069